"I'm sure everything appeared the way you said."

Keir added fiercely, "Was *made* to appear that way."

"Made to!" Abigail tried to follow what he was saying.

"Abigail, I've been doing a lot of thinking this last week since I learned what happened to you. I know *I* wasn't driving my car that day, and I'm ninety-nine percent certain who was. I can prove it, but I need your cooperation."

He spoke as if it mattered to him, but she had meant little enough to him a year ago — his continuing affair with another woman and his impatient ending of their engagement had proved that. But Abigail found it mattered to *her*.

"What do you want me to do?" Doubt and uncertainty was reflected in her eyes.

"I want you to trust me."

Books by Stacy Absalom

HARLEQUIN ROMANCE
2581—KNAVE OF HEARTS
2671—THE PASSION AND THE PAIN
2689—DARK NIGHT DAWNING

These books may be available at your local bookseller.

Dark Night Dawning

Stacy Absalom

Harlequin Books

TORONTO • NEW YORK • LONDON
AMSTERDAM • PARIS • SYDNEY • HAMBURG
STOCKHOLM • ATHENS • TOKYO • MILAN

Original hardcover edition published in 1984
by Mills & Boon Limited

ISBN 0-373-02689-7

Harlequin Romance first edition May 1985

CHAPTER ONE

THE taxi drew up outside Dornfield House and Abigail gave an involuntary shiver as the vague sense of foreboding that had dogged her ever since Serge had sprung this 'surprise' outing on her intensified. She suddenly wanted to beg him to take her back to Chelsea and let them spend the evening quietly together rather than attend this celebrity concert Lady Elizabeth Dornfield—that indefatigable party giver and patron of music—was putting on in the ballroom of her London home. But Serge looked so pleased with himself as he handed her out of the cab, his grey hair blowing untidily in the cool wind, so proud as he straightened his stooped shoulders to lead her in on his arm, that she kept silent.

Dear Serge. What would she have done without his loving support, his gentle bullying, his faith in her ability to pick up the shattered pieces of her life? Not for anything in the world would she hurt his feelings when he had been such a good friend. He wasn't to know this place could resurrect memories she would far rather forget. He only saw her as revisiting at last one of her old stamping grounds, returning to the world where she had once belonged. Once. . . .

Once she had been a regular visitor to this house, sometimes as a performer and sometimes as a celebrity guest, but that had been another lifetime, when she had been a successful and much fêted young concert pianist. Once she had believed herself to be loved, and it hadn't been Serge's arm she had clung to.

Fiercely Abigail pushed that painfully stirring memory back into the deep pit to which she had consigned all such memories these last twelve months.

5

She had thought the wound had healed but tonight she was learning the scar tissue was still too sensitive to be touched.

She had thought she had come to terms with the fact that never again would the music of long dead composers speak beneath her agile fingers. Never again would she experience that expectant hush before she touched the keys or hear that elating applause when her performance was over. But now, as she reluctantly mounted the steps of Dornfield House on Serge's arm, she realised it had been one thing to accept the unpalatable truth back home in her isolated cottage where she rarely saw anyone and where the sheer struggle for survival took up most of her energies, but quite another to be faced with the reality of it like this.

It was surprisingly painful, being reduced to a nonentity when once she had been a shining star. A blow to her pride, she supposed. But she knew it went deeper than that. It was being brought face to face with the fact that she no longer belonged in this world which was the only one she knew. She would never be more now than an anonymous member of a concert audience offering her applause to others.

Expecting to find the entrance hall thronged with people, Abigail was puzzled to find it almost deserted except for a small group in conversation at the far end. Serge paused to lift the satin-lined cloak from her shoulders and hand it to the maid waiting to receive it, and the first intimation that tonight she was to be anything but anonymous came when a well-bred voice boomed out, 'Abigail, my dear, it's so good to see you again!' and a lady of indeterminate age and amazonian proportions detached herself from the small group and swept forward across the marble floor, her hands outstretched.

'Lady Elizabeth. . . .' Abigail murmured, surprised at being singled out by her hostess for a personal greeting.

'Thank you so much for coming.' Lady Elizabeth put a scented cheek against hers.

'Thank you for asking me,' Abigail responded politely.

Lady Elizabeth's booming laugh rang out. 'My dear girl, I've been pestering Serge to let me do this for ages but he wouldn't hear of it until he was sure you were up to it. As it is I've been on thorns in case you changed your mind.'

Seeing Abigail's eyes widen in bewildered alarm Lady Elizabeth said accusingly, 'You haven't told her what it's all about then, Serge?'

'My dear Elizabeth, if I had, you would never have got your wish.' Serge took Abigail's hand. 'As it is I can only hope this young woman will forgive me for tricking her like this and not punish me by withdrawing her friendship.' His voice had never quite lost its Russian accent even after more than half a lifetime of living in London, and at moments of deep emotion the accent always thickened.

It sounded very Russian now and added to Abigail's creeping apprehension. 'Tricking me! Serge, I don't understand.'

'All shall be revealed!' Before Serge could answer Lady Elizabeth had taken her arm and was sweeping her inexorably across the hall towards the small group she had recently left. 'Come and meet the reception committee.'

Before Abigail's stunned gaze the group separated into recognisable figures. The first to shake her hand and murmur a greeting was Raphael Andre, the eminent conductor, and then she was passed to Ling Tan, the young Chinese pianist whose talent Abigail had always admired and whose boyish shyness and difficulty with English had always aroused her sympathy.

'Abigail, darling! We were beginning to think we'd never pull this off.' Now she was being hugged by

Dorinda Clay who had been her closest friend at music college and who was much in demand now as a solo cellist, while James Stevens, who had also been a fellow student, beamed at her widely.

'We were all shattered when we heard about your accident, Abby,' he said, 'and we thought this was the best way we could help.'

Abigail stared from one to the other in utter bewilderment. 'I haven't the faintest idea what you're talking about! What *is* going on?'

Dorinda opened her mouth to rush in with an explanation but Lady Elizabeth broke in, 'There's no time now. We're keeping everyone waiting.'

She swept towards the massive double doors that led into the ballroom and as she thrust them dramatically open the sight that met Abigail's eyes stunned her into numbed incredulity. The ballroom was packed with row on row of small chairs, every one of them occupied and every occupant turning expectantly to look at her as they rose to their feet and began to applaud. It took a moment or two before she realised they were applauding *her*.

Abigail was suddenly overwhelmingly conscious that the black, full-skirted chiffon dress she wore was old, a relic of her former life when she had needed such gowns to appear in public, and that the village dressmaker's attempts to take it in to fit her had been less than expert. All those eyes trained on her made her humiliatingly aware of the weight she had lost, the boniness the neckline of the dress did little to conceal and the skinniness of her arms through the diaphanous material of the long sleeves.

Involuntarily her hand went up to smooth her honey gold hair—swept up tonight into a gleaming coil on the crown of her head—until she realised it was her black gloved left hand she had raised. Self-consciously she let it fall and hid it among the folds of her skirt. How could Serge have done this to her, put her on show like a freak at a fair? she wondered.

But the smiling audience saw nothing freakish. They saw a girl of heartbreaking fragility, slender almost to the point of emaciation, whose waist could have been spanned by the two hands of almost any man in the room and whose graceful neck looked as if it was not strong enough to support the gleaming weight of her hair. A beautiful girl whose magnolia pallor and dark, haunted eyes made her look far younger than her twenty-five years.

The expressionless mask she had schooled herself for many months now to withdraw behind slipped and her soft mouth was suddenly vulnerable, the dark eyes she turned to her elderly escort filled with panic. 'Serge. . . .'

He patted the hand resting on his arm, his wise, lined face full of compassion. 'Relax, my dear. Everyone here is your friend and wishes you well.'

Those in the audience near enough to witness her instinctive dependence on her old teacher were touched, all save one dark, tall, frowning man.

And when Abigail still seemed frozen into immobility Serge pleaded, 'My dear, don't deprive your friends of this chance to show you how much you mean to them.'

Lady Elizabeth was already sailing confidently up the gangway between the rows of chairs and Abigail knew she would be making an even bigger fool of herself if she turned and ran as every instinct prompted her to do. Gathering her remoteness around her like a veil to hide her shock she allowed Serge to lead her forward through the still applauding audience to the row of chairs right at the front. Numbly she sat in the seat indicated and blindly took the programme Serge handed to her.

It wasn't until the audience had settled back into its seats and the orchestra on the platform had broken into the overture from Mozart's *Don Giovanni* that Abigail glanced at the programme on her lap, and then the elegant print on the cover seemed to dance before her eyes. *The Abigail Paston Benefit Concert.*

At last some of the remarks made to her by Lady Elizabeth and her two former college friends began to make sense. She turned wide, reproachful eyes on Serge. He grimaced and whispered, 'I'm sorry. Maybe I *should* have told you. . . .'

And if he had, nothing would have dragged her here tonight, she acknowledged silently. Oh they meant well, all these former friends and colleagues. She was touched by their gesture, by their eagerness to help, but there was humiliation too, knowing herself to be an object of charity.

She hadn't been able to avoid this visit to London as she'd had an appointment with the surgeon for a check up on her damaged hand, but she could have made the trip from the cottage and back in a day, if only she hadn't listened to Serge's blandishments.

'Let's make it an occasion,' he'd written in one of the letters that had been her only contact with the world of music since her injury.

> '*Make an old man happy and come and stay with me, at least for a few days. I'll arrange a visit to your music publisher for you. Mr Bowers was delighted with that first collection of studies for students you did for them and if you've completed the second volume you could deliver it to him yourself. I'll get a couple of tickets for a concert too, so bring along a glamorous dress.*'

And because Serge had always been so good to her, she had agreed.

Serge Markovitch had been one of her tutors at music college and quite the severest taskmaster there, but Abigail had never minded how hard she worked for him. Right from the beginning there had been a rapport between the young girl and the elderly man, he recognising at once not only the technical brilliance of her talent but also the underlying sensitivity and capacity for passion, she responding like a dry sponge to water, readily soaking up all he could teach her, eager to profit from his wisdom and wealth of experience.

He had retired from the faculty of the college at the end of her first year there but by then she was already having private lessons with him at his Chelsea home. Even after her professional career had begun to blossom and flourish they had kept in close touch with each other, Abigail sending him tickets for all her London concerts and writing to him when she was on tour, visiting the Chelsea house whenever she was able, sometimes for the benefit of his help and advice when she was adding some new work to her repertoire, sometimes just for the pleasure of seeing him.

She had been too shocked to be aware of it at the time but later she had learned it was Serge who'd had her transferred from the local hospital where the emergency services had taken her after the accident to a London clinic where he had put her under the care of one of the best surgeons in the country. Not that it had been any use. Her career was just as surely in ruins even if Sir Justin Chalmers had made a better job of piecing her hand together than any other surgeon might have done.

It had been Serge who had taken charge of Granny Lucy, bringing her to London and installing her in his own home so she would be on hand for hospital visiting, bolstering the shocked and distraught old lady with his kindness and optimism, and it had been Serge's quiet voice at her bedside hour after agonised hour that had kept Abigail sane when the necessity of keeping the true enormity of what had happened locked inside her had pushed her close to the brink.

Serge had seen to everything, cancelling the arrangements for the wedding that was no longer going to take place, dealing with her agent to cancel all her

professional engagements, helping her to answer the
letters of commiseration, disposing of the lease of her
London flat, persistently and tirelessly trying to break
through her zombie-like state of shock. When she was
finally released from hospital he had taken her to his
house in Chelsea and had tried to persuade her to stay
on in London with him, tried to make her think of the
future, suggesting she should channel her talents into
teaching now her career as a performer was irrevocably
over, even offering to let her take over some of his
pupils.

But for Abigail in her agonised state of mind there
was no future. The past had ceased to have any
meaning and the future became non-existent the
moment the black Porsche had tried to run her down.
So when it became obvious Granny Lucy—who
seemed to have aged twenty years in a few weeks and
who was suddenly frail and defeated—was eating her
heart out to go back home, Abigail had accompanied
her in the hire-car arranged by Serge. Mill House
where Granny Lucy had brought her up after her
parents' tragic death had once been a place of safety
and security for her, and when the news reached them
on the village grapevine that Marmion—the house
which was to have been her home after her
marriage—was up for sale, a little of that old feeling
of security came back.

But not for long. Only two weeks after their return to
Mill House, Granny Lucy had died quietly in her sleep.
And once again it was Serge who stepped in to take
charge, making arrangements for the funeral, renewing
his persuasive arguments when her grandmother had
finally been laid to rest in the village churchyard that
Abigail should go back to London to make her home
with him, arguments that were redoubled when he
learned that all Granny Lucy's capital had been
expended on Abigail's musical training and that, as her
pension died with her, there was no way Abigail was

going to be able to afford to go on living at Mill House now she no longer had an income of her own.

But this second crushing blow in so short a time had the effect of dragging Abigail out of her anaesthetised state. The thought of going back to London when *he* might be there filled her with panic. Oh common sense told her that London was a big place and that the chances of their paths crossing again were remote, but after the unbelievable thing he had tried to do to her, the thought of being within miles of him chilled her to the soul. Only here in Great Wiston did she even begin to feel safe, especially as Marmion now had a new owner.

It was the vicar who solved her problem. Dodie's Retreat was a row of cottages built at the turn of the century to house retired hosiery workers but as it was so far out of the village, few elderly people cared to live there in spite of the low rents when the local council could house them more comfortably in the village itself, with the result that the cottages were mostly let off to university students during term time. But the vicar, in his capacity as trustee of the Retreat had offered her one of the cottages on a permanent basis and she had accepted it gratefully. It was rather primitive with few of the amenities of her grandmother's house. A bathroom had been made out of the smaller of the two bedrooms but the only lavatory was housed across the small back yard, and the old-fashioned range in the kitchen was the only form of heating, providing hot water from its back boiler and cooking facilities in its side oven. But furnished with some of her grandmother's pieces it had been comfortable enough, and with the proceeds from the sale of Mill House invested it brought in enough income for her to live on as long as she was careful.

Frugal was perhaps a better word, Abigail grimaced, joining in the applause at the end of the Mozart overture and at the appearance of James Stevens,

Dorinda Clay and Ling Tan on to the platform to begin
Beethoven's Triple Concerto for violin, cello and piano
without it really impinging on her train of thought,
because even with the small extra income added to her
tight budget by the few pupils she taught and the
publishing of her collection of piano studies for
students, it was sometimes a straight choice between
eating and meeting some unexpected expense like the
cost of her train fare for this trip to London.

Serge of course had been upset by her decision to
take the cottage and when he'd taken himself back to
London in high dudgeon she had worried in case he
meant to wash his hands of her. But she had done him
an injustice. Twice a week he had written to her, long,
newsy letters, caring letters that had made her feel she
was not utterly alone and forgotten. Letters full of the
old man's wit and wisdom, so that reading them was
like having him at her elbow talking to her. Letters that
became the highspot of her existence, eagerly anticipated, read and reread with a lingering savour. Letters
full of encouragement and sometimes not without
criticism, because of course when she began to write
music of her own she had sent him the scores.

At first she suspected his delighted encouragement
was merely a sop to her shattered self-confidence, that
he was trying to boost her morale and would have
praised any rubbish she turned out. But when her first
book of piano studies had been completed to his
satisfaction and had promptly been accepted for
publication, she was forced to believe his praise was
sincere and the boost to her confidence had prompted
her to try something more ambitious. That was when
she had learned his criticism could be every bit as
scathing as it had been during her student days. But
though he pulled no punches, his criticism was always
constructive, never destructive, and she had welcomed it
and responded to it with even greater efforts because it
proved to her he was taking her first stumbling efforts

at musical composition seriously. Not that she ever expected to hear her Prelude performed, unless she could persuade Serge to play it for her while she was in London.

Another wave of applause rose up round her and Abigail realised the Triple Concerto had come to an end without her hearing a note. Feeling guilty she joined in the appreciative clamour as the three soloists took their bows and when, after the third recall, Dorinda and James retired and the orchestra relaxed while Ling Tan resumed his place at the piano, she was aware of a murmur of anticipation rising through the audience. And as the notes of the opening bars cascaded from Ling Tan's flying fingers Abigail jolted upright in her seat, her attention riveted in incredulous recognition.

Serge reached across and squeezed her hand and her wide-eyed gaze flew to his smiling face. Without speaking he opened the programme on her lap and pointed, and there it was in black and white, the last item, Prelude by Abigail Paston.

Her Prelude! Ling Tan was playing it in front of a room full of some of the most distinguished and influential figures in the musical world.

Abigail knew every note, having lived for so many months with the music inside her head, but hearing it played was an indescribable experience. She listened avidly, hardly breathing, her eyes fixed on the slight young man at the piano, admiring and inwardly applauding his technique, especially his effortless execution of the parts she knew would be difficult. To her it sounded wonderful, but she knew she didn't have the objectivity to distinguish whether it was really any good.

When the final notes died away there was a breathless hush and then the applause broke like a clap of thunder. Brimming over with gratitude towards Ling Tan for paying her the compliment of playing her work

Abigail applauded as enthusiastically as any as the
young pianist took his bow. But instead of retiring to
the wings before coming forward to take another bow
Ling Tan stepped down from the platform, his hand
outstretched towards her. Abigail felt Serge push her
forward out of her seat and before she quite realised
what was happening she too was standing on the
platform, sharing the soloist's acclaim.

Holding her hand Ling Tan lifted her arm high in the
air then swept it down in a bow before standing back, a
wide grin on his face, to add his own appreciation to
that of the audience, and then as if sensing how
overwhelmed she was, he stepped forward again to hug
her. The first scattered bravos rose to a concerted roar.
Touched and elated at this evidence that she still had a
place in this world she had thought was lost to her,
Abigail struggled against the painful lump in her throat
and the prick of tears in her eyes that blurred the sea of
faces.

When it seemed the audience was never going to let
her go, Lady Elizabeth surged up on to the platform
and imperiously raised her hand.

'Ladies and gentlemen . . .' she boomed, 'I don't wish
to make this occasion any more of an ordeal for our
guest of honour than I need. As you can see, Abigail is
already in a state of shock and you'll understand why
when I tell you she had no idea when she arrived here
this evening that this concert was for her benefit, or that
one of her own works was to be performed.

'Abigail, my dear . . .' Lady Elizabeth turned to her,
her voice softening perceptibly, 'we hope you'll forgive
us for springing this on you but everyone in this
room—and many, many more who couldn't possibly be
accommodated—wanted so much to have this opportunity of expressing our sincere sympathy in your
misfortune. You've been sadly missed, my dear, and it's
heartbreaking to know you'll never be able to play for
us again. But we hope this will make it a little easier for

you to establish yourself in your new career—writing music instead of performing it.' She handed Abigail a slip of paper.

Her colour coming and going in waves Abigail stared dazedly at the cheque in her hand, hardly aware of the storm of applause or of the popping flashbulbs of the press. It was for several thousand pounds! She bit her lip, tears rising thickly in her throat.

She was still struggling for composure when the applause finally died to an expectant hush and she realised with rising panic that she was expected to make some response. Her frightened glance flew at once to Serge on the front row and his calm smile did much to reassure her. Persuading Ling Tan to perform her work must have been Serge's doing; she couldn't repay him by breaking down.

'I—I don't know what to say,' she began shakily, 'except thank you. Thank you, Ling Tan——' she turned to the smiling young man '—for playing my music. It's the first time I've heard it and there are not words enough to tell you what it meant to me. And thank you all——' she turned back to the audience '—for your overwhelming generosity. I—I never realised I had so many wonderful friends.' Emotion finally overcame her and she choked on a sob.

Once again a wave of clapping made the glittering prisms on the chandeliers tremble. Ling Tan helped her down from the platform to where Serge waited for her and they followed in Lady Elizabeth's wake through the ranks of the now standing audience back to the big double doors. Once out in the spacious hall Abigail allowed her shoulders to slump in relief, but she quickly realised her ordeal was not yet over when her hostess said, 'A little supper now, my dear. There are so many people who want to talk to you.'

The sense of foreboding that had dogged her earlier returned and she looked up at her escort pleadingly. 'Serge . . . must I?'

'Yes, you must.' Serge's pale blue eyes were compassionate but his grip on her arm drew her inexorably up the sweeping staircase after their hostess. 'My dearest girl,' he said quietly, 'you've taken a giant step tonight. You've proved that though Abigail Paston the concert pianist is dead, Abigail Paston the composer has risen from her ashes. Very few of your sex have achieved success in this field but tonight you've made a beginning. If you are to go on to greater things you must face the judgment of your peers, meet people who can help you, learn from the criticism of those whose opinion you respect.' His lined face softened into an encouraging smile. 'You said just now you didn't know you had so many friends. Don't shut them out of your life, my dear.'

Abigail flushed at his gentle reprimand but knew it was deserved. All these months shut away in her isolated cottage had made her selfish, too wrapped up in her own need to hide away from the world before it could inflict any more damage on her. She took a deep breath to still her inner trembling and followed Lady Elizabeth into the drawing room where she accepted a glass of champagne.

The drawing room of Dornfield House was almost as large as the ballroom on the ground floor but it quickly filled up as it seemed that everyone who had been in the audience tonight wanted to speak to her, to show their delight at having her back among them, showering her with compliments over the successful beginning to her new career as a composer of serious music. At first Serge stayed supportively at her side as they moved from group to group and Abigail was unaware of the exact moment he deserted her. She was talking to Ling Tan when she realised her old friend was no longer beside her, but she felt only a momentary anxiety. The champagne she had been sipping, the warmth shown her by former colleagues and friends, and most of all Ling Tan's shy modesty when she congratulated him on his performance relaxed her tension and blunted her earlier apprehension.

For quite some time they discussed her Prelude and his interpretation of it, until they were joined by the austere figure of Raphael Andre, the conductor known for his acerbic tongue and uncompromising expectations of excellence. Abigail had worked with him on numerous occasions as a pianist and valued his opinion above all others, and as his piercing eyes probed the cool mask she wore as a defence, she waited in trepidation for his verdict.

'A brilliant piece of work, Abigail,' he said at last, and she let out a long breath. But her relief and pleasure were premature as he went on, 'But where was all the passion and feeling you used to put into your performances? Your Prelude had all the brilliance of a perfectly cut diamond, but it lacked a diamond's inner fire.'

Before she could even begin to react to his judgment a voice behind her said, 'My own feelings exactly.'

The odd foreboding that had dogged her all evening crystallised at the sound of that once familiar voice with the trace of Canadian accent and she knew that this was what she had been fearing, even though she hadn't seen or heard from him since that last terrifying glimpse through the darkly tinted car windscreen and had every reason to suppose he feared meeting her as much as she feared meeting him.

She whirled round, her face draining of colour. Still as tanned and virilely attractive as ever; dark brown hair a little longer than she remembered it but still crisp and vital, the small scar at the right hand corner of his upper lip—which he had once told her was a legacy of a lumber camp brawl—giving a cynical upturn to his unsmiling mouth. The perfectly cut dinner jacket could not conceal the threatening power of his broad shoulders as he towered over her, nor did the tiny lines etched into the skin at the corners of his eyes soften their steel grey hardness.

Keir Minto. The man she had once loved with all her heart and soul and senses, with all the abandon of her deeply passionate nature. The man who had carelessly turned that love and trust into pain and uncertainty until he had cruelly thrown it back in her face with an accusation of obsessive jealousy. The man who had finally and senselessly staged that nightmare trap that had robbed her of her livelihood and had been intended to rob her of her life.

The shock of seeing him again turned to sheer terror, drying her mouth while at the same time every pore oozed cold perspiration; a terror so profound there was no hiding it. It stopped her breath, froze her white face and leapt from her dilated eyes. She saw his brows draw together in a questioning frown but like a mesmerised rabbit she was unable to tear her gaze away from the source of danger.

As if from a far distance she heard Raphael Andre saying, 'Only if you can recapture that inner fire you once had will you ever produce work of lasting merit.'

She could not really take in what he was saying but at least his voice had broken through her paralysis of fear. The defensive shutter came down, wiping her face clear of expression. She turned back to the eminent conductor to apologise for her inattention but he was already moving away. And somehow, without her knowing how he did it, Keir had manoeuvred himself between her and the crowd, isolating her, and once again the sick panic flared.

'For God's sake stop looking at me as if I was Frankenstein's monster!' he ground out, gripping her arm and trapping her more firmly in the corner. 'I only want to talk to you—find out how you've been since——' He bit the sentence off as Abigail shook so violently the champagne in her glass spilt over her hand and down her dress.

He took the glass from her and put it on a table but didn't release the painful grip on her arm. 'What the hell have you been doing to yourself? Your nerves are shot to pieces and there's less flesh on you than there is on a sparrow.' The grip slackened almost to a caress and gasping incredulously at his question, she jerked away from his touch.

She saw his eyes harden as she remained dumb. 'I asked you what you've done to yourself to get into this state,' he demanded again, his voice harsh though he made no new attempt to touch her.

Abigail tried frantically to see past him, praying for Serge to come and rescue her, but Keir's powerful body blocked her view. And anyway, what could a gentle old man of seventy do against a cold-blooded monster only half his age? she wondered despairingly. All right, so Keir hadn't actually succeeded in his monstrous intent but it hadn't been for want of trying. Then somebody nearby laughed and she took courage from the sheer normality of the sound. Even if she couldn't see them there were people still close at hand, lots of people. So what could Keir do to her here, in front of a roomful of witnesses?

'I've done nothing to myself,' she said tonelessly, keeping her eyes fixed on his shirt front. What did he want of her, seeking her out again after all this time? Not to ask after her state of health, that was for sure!

He made an exasperated sound. 'Don't give me that! When I last saw you you were perfectly fit, and now you look like the victim of a famine.'

Abigail drew in her breath sharply, her body rigid, the memory of that final nightmare betrayal—the car hurtling towards her with Keir at the wheel—leaping out of its burial place. 'The last time you saw me you didn't wait to find out whether I was alive or dead, so don't pretend you care now,' she said between clenched teeth.

The bitter accusation was met with silence but she could not bring herself to look at his face, afraid of

seeing the knowledge of what he had done in his eyes.
Then, 'I knew you were upset when I broke our
engagement,' he clipped out, 'but not even someone as
possessive as you can actually die of a broken heart.'

Possessive. Even now the injustice of that accusation
could hurt. Had it been possessiveness to object to his
continued blatant association with his mistress even
while he was planning marriage to herself?

'I'm not talking about you breaking our engagement,
and you know it,' she said in a shaking voice. Her left
hand ached and throbbed as it had not done for
months, as if the damaged bones and nerves and
tendons were remembering past agonies.

'Then what *are* you talking about?' he demanded
impatiently. He gripped her shoulders again and for a
moment she thought he was going to shake her. She
shrank from his touch and Keir's lip curled contemptuously. 'Anyway it didn't take you long to get over our
break-up, did it? You soon found yourself a replace-
ment. Oh yes, news travels,' he jeered at her blank
expression.

Abigail blinked, trying to make sense of what he was
saying. Seeing him at all had thrown her into panicky
confusion and now it seemed he was trying to confuse
her further. 'I—I don't know what you mean.'

'It comes as a surprise that I was worried about the
way I'd left you?' His dark eyebrows rose sardonically,
and she gasped at his sheer hypocrisy.

'After what you did? Yes!'

'If you'd really known me it wouldn't surprise you.
But you never did really know me, did you Abigail?' He
hunched his powerful shoulders in irritation. 'I made
enquiries, asked someone to check up on you, find out
how you were, what you were doing.'

It was like icy water being trickled down her spine,
the knowledge that he had set someone to spy on her.
'Why?' Unguardedly she looked up into his face, licking
her dry lips. 'Why did you want to know?'

His expression was unreadable and a muscle twitched on his jaw. 'Why do you think?'

Her dark eyes widened again in fear, her heart pounding so hard it seemed to shake her whole frame. He'd had someone follow her, watch her, perhaps to finish off what he'd failed to do at the first attempt?

'Please . . . haven't you done enough?' Her voice was a thin, frightened thread. 'If you're worried that I'll give you away, you needn't be. I didn't tell the police at the time who was driving the car and I don't intend to tell them, ever.'

'Car? What car? You're talking in riddles, girl.'

Abigail could have sworn the bafflement on his face was genuine, but then twelve months ago she could have sworn Keir Minto was incapable of the appalling act he'd attempted. She stared at him dumbly. If it wasn't an assurance of her silence he was after, then what *did* he want? Why was he playing this cruel cat and mouse game?

'So quit stalling, Abigail.' His hands gripped the tender flesh of her upper arms painfully. 'The first mention of your name I've heard since I got back to England six months ago and it's for this benefit concert tonight. So now I *have* found you I want some straight answers. What's this accident everyone keeps whispering about? Was it really so bad you had to throw up a successful career and start *writing* music when you were so much better at playing it? What happened to you, Abigail?'

'You have the gall to ask me that?' Bitter anger at his duplicity conquered her fear. 'All right, so you didn't wait to see how much damage you'd done but you must have read about it in the papers. I'm told it made the nationals even though I was in no condition to read it for myself. You must have known you'd ruined my career. Even the most brilliant pianist needs *two* hands.' Her bitter rage gave her strength and raising both her arms she knocked his restraining hands violently away.

His eyes were drawn at once to the black glove she had successfully kept hidden till now. 'Your hand! You damaged your hand?'

But the force of her push had brought them both farther out of the corner and she heard Serge's kindly voice saying, 'So there you are my dear. I was beginning to think you'd reneged and gone home without me.'

Almost sobbing with relief Abigail moved closer to the old man's side, slipping her hand through his arm and clinging to him.

'Won't you introduce me to your—friend, Abigail?' Keir's request was polite enough but there was hard anger underlying his voice and the slight pause before the word 'friend' was designed to be insulting.

With Serge's support and now in full view of everyone in the room she could afford to ignore Keir's bristling threat. She lifted her chin. 'This is Serge Markovitch, my former teacher and dearest friend.'

Keir's eyes bored into her as if he would pierce the features schooled now into her habitual cool remoteness. 'As Abigail doesn't seem inclined to complete the introduction I'll have to do it myself,' he drawled, holding out his hand. 'I'm Keir Minto, Abigail's former fiancé.'

'So *you're* the man who once lit this girl up like a neon sign!' Serge took the proffered hand, his bushy eyebrows lifting in surprise, his keen glance assessing the younger man. 'I don't know what happened between you to extinguish that light,' he went on dryly, 'but I could have wished you were still around at the time of her accident. If she ever needed you, it was then.'

'No!' Abigail quivered with the vehemence of her denial. 'He was the last man on earth I needed. I only wanted to forget he had ever been born!'

If she hadn't known Keir was a superb actor she might have been taken in by the sudden flinching pain he pretended. She swayed, feeling sick and drained, exhausted by the conflicting emotions, by the strange undercurrents, the tormenting, appalling memories. 'Serge, can't we go home now?' she pleaded piteously. 'Please. . . .'

And taking one look at her desperate pallor he patted her hand. 'Of course, my dear. Goodnight, Mr Minto.' He turned her away.

'Abigail. . . .' She heard Keir call after her but she didn't look back.

She was still shaking as Serge helped her out of the cab outside his narrow old house in Chelsea that had been almost a home from home for her since her student days. Now, after all the shocks and tensions of the evening, it seemed more of a refuge than ever. While Serge fumbled with the key she found herself glancing fearfully over her shoulder in case Keir—like some inexorable Nemesis intent on revenge for some sin she didn't even know she had committed—should have followed her, and when the door was finally open she almost fell inside.

The first-floor sitting room was warm, heavy red curtains drawn closely across the windows shutting out the night and all its terrors. Red-shaded lamps cast a rosy glow and the flickering simulated flames of the gas fire added a homely touch, but still Abigail shivered. Solicitously the old man took her cloak and pressed her into a chair by the fire.

'I see Mrs Price has left us a tray as she promised.' He unscrewed the thermos jug and poured out two cups of milky cocoa and then coaxed her to eat a couple of his housekeeper's dainty sandwiches.

The hot drink dispelled some of the chill that gripped her but she was still tense, waiting for the expected questions about her meeting with Keir. But to her relief Serge didn't comment on it, talking instead of the concert, passing on some of the comments people had made concerning her own Prelude. 'You were surprised to find it part of the programme?' he finished.

'Surprised!' Abigail smiled at him. 'I nearly fell off my chair! I'd no idea you'd shown the score to anyone else. You never mentioned it.'

Serge's eyes twinkled impishly. 'You don't begrudge an old man indulging in a bit of clever meddling, do you?' He leaned forward in his chair eagerly. 'I could see Ling Tan was interested when I mentioned to him you'd written a work that would be ideal for inclusion in the programme. And when I also happened to mention to Mr Bowers—your publisher—that Ling Tan was eager to give the first performance on such a widely publicised occasion if only there could be copies produced in time. . . .' He gave a complacent shrug.

'You mean it's been published too?' Abigail squeaked.

He reached across to a side table, picked up a slim score and tossed it into her lap, grinning triumphantly. 'Such an opportunity to let the world know what you're doing now was too good to miss.'

Abigail fingered the copy of her first printed serious work and felt a deep thrill. 'And you never breathed a word,' she said softly.

Looking complacent, Serge settled back in his chair. 'By that time I'd developed a taste for intrigue. Besides, I didn't dare tell you. I wasn't at all sure even the opportunity to hear your own work performed would be enough to get you to that concert if you got wind of what it was in aid of. You've forgiven me? It wasn't *such* an ordeal?' The kindly eyes regarded her quizzically and Abigail had to suppress a shudder. He would never know just how much of an ordeal it had been. Oh not the concert itself, but afterwards. . . .

To blot out the memory of Keir Minto's threatening presence she said, 'Raphael Andre told me my work had no inner fire.'

At once Serge's complacent expression disappeared and he frowned. 'That man can be blunt to the point of brutality.'

'So you agree with him?'

He said carefully, 'It's true your misfortunes have quenched your spirit and it shows in your work, in spite of the technical brilliance. But don't worry, my dear, it will come back. You're young and resilient and one day your real nature will reassert itself. You'll come alive, begin to *live* again.' He hesitated and then plunged on, 'That young man you were talking to tonight ... there's no chance he might be able to rekindle the spark in you again?'

This time Abigail couldn't hide the shudder. 'No, never!'

Serge sighed with regret. 'Of course not. There's nothing so dead as the ashes of an old love. But there'll be other loves for you, Abigail. It's as inevitable as the sunrise.' He rose to his feet and for the first time Abigail noticed how tired and drawn he was.

He escorted her up the second flight of stairs to her room. 'Goodnight, my child. Sleep well.' Dropping a fatherly kiss on her forehead he pushed her gently through the door.

Other loves? Oh no, Serge was wrong. Abigail wrapped her thin arms across her breast protectively as his footsteps receded down the passage. She never intended to let anyone get close enough to hurt her as Keir had done. He had inflicted enough pain to last her several lifetimes. Safer to shut herself away in her cottage with her work than risk another devastating misjudgment of character. Better this half life with her feelings locked securely away than to trust in any man's love again.

She crossed the room and jeered at her reflection in the mirror. Love! Keir had never loved her. Oh for a time he'd been convincing, making her believe he was as deeply and irrevocably in love with her as she was with him. So deeply, she thought with bitter cynicism, that even while he was urging her to make whatever changes she wished to his home in preparation for their marriage, he was still pursuing his affair with his mistress. So irrevocably that when she'd voiced her protest he'd broken off their engagement, calling her unreasonably and obsessively jealous.

How could she have been such a bad judge of character as to be taken in by him, a man who had proved himself to be so cold-blooded and ruthless as to set up that diabolical trap to destroy her?

Abigail slumped on to the dressing-table stool and buried her face in her hands. Why? Why had Keir made that deliberate and utterly senseless attempt on her life? It was a question that had haunted her for twelve months, perhaps would go on haunting her all her life. Because she had attempted to see him just one more time, refusing to believe he could turn his back on her so casually after all they had shared? Had he been afraid she would make a nuisance of herself? Had that carefully staged 'accident' been his final, ruthless solution to ridding himself of her for good?

She lowered her hands and stared at her own frightened eyes reflected in the mirror, because now there was an even more important question burning into her mind. Why had Keir appeared again after so long? Why had he come back into her life as she was beginning to climb out of the abyss into which he had thrust her?

CHAPTER TWO

SLOWLY, with reluctant dragging movements, Abigail got ready for bed, but at last huddled beneath the comforting duvet sleep was aeons away. Every time she closed her eyes Keir's face rose up before her, at first as he'd been tonight, hard-eyed and subtly threatening, but as if the shock of seeing him again had uncovered memories she had long interred without a headstone, the mental picture changed, softened into the way he had been in the early days of their courtship.

She fought against the resurgence of these memories, switching on the bedside lamp and trying vainly to read, but like the contents of Pandora's box, once the lid had been lifted, no power in earth or heaven could prevent them flying free.

Keir as she had seen him the very first time, outstanding even in that well-heeled and sophisticated crowd, formally dressed in an impeccably cut dark grey suit and yet still giving the impression that he would be equally at home on the open prairies. Toronto, that had been, the first concert of her Canadian tour, one of the biggest audiences she had ever performed before and the most wildly enthusiastic reception she'd ever received.

It had been a gruelling programme she had set herself, Mozart's Piano Concerto in E flat major in the first half and the Beethoven Emperor Concerto after the interval, and she had naturally been nervous. And yet the instant she seated herself at the piano she felt the warm goodwill flowing from the crowded auditorium and something magical had taken place. Something inside her responded to that warmth and, her nervousness forgotten, she poured her whole self into

her music. And wrung out and perspiring as she was
when the last chords died away, their standing ovation
had lifted her high on a surge of elation like nothing she
had experienced before.

She was still flying high as a kite at the reception
after the concert where she was to meet musicians,
music lovers and the cream of Toronto society. The
large room was crowded and the noise level punishing
but the experience of being fêted like a true celebrity
instead of merely a promising beginner was heady.
And if she was wise enough to take with a pinch of
salt the extravagant compliments showered on her as
she was steered from group to group by a short,
balding, rather pompous man who seemed to have
designated himself her guide and mentor, it didn't
stop her enjoying them.

And then suddenly he was standing there before her,
a tall man, well over six feet with a breadth of shoulder
that made every other man in the room look puny.
Thick, dark brown hair brushed casually back only to
spring forward again over a broad brow and a tan that
looked as if it owed more to a life spent outdoors than
to one acquired over a few weeks at one of the world's
sunspots. Too rugged to be strictly handsome, the hard
planes of his face running from strong cheekbones to
square chin were still undeniably attractive and the little
scar on his upper lip at the right hand side of his firm,
clear cut mouth gave a look of humour to what might
otherwise have been an austere expression. But it was
his eyes that riveted her attention. Grey eyes under level
dark brows, clear grey eyes that captured her own gaze
and would not let it go, until the noise, the pressing
crush receded and it was as if they were alone. Held
inexorably by that gaze she swayed, involuntarily
putting out her hands towards him.

He took them in his own and she was able to draw
breath again as his eyes released her to look down, but
only to find herself quivering at his touch. He flattened

his palms, looking down at her short-nailed, long-fingered, deceptively delicate looking hands.

'Incredible that they should have such power,' he said, and his voice was attractively deep, more English than any she had heard that night but still with a slight Canadian intonation.

'You're a musician too?' The words came out breathily as his hands closed round hers again and those amazingly clear eyes came back to her face.

He shook his head, the corners of his mouth curling into a rueful smile. 'I learned to play the piano after a fashion but I'm more at home handling a chain saw.'

'You're talking to Keir Minto, one of our country's most successful businessmen, Abigail,' her self-appointed host said importantly. 'Lumber, farming, minerals, electronics ... you name it, he's got a finger in it.'

Abigail blinked. Undoubtedly he looked successful but wasn't he too young to be *that* successful? Not more than his mid thirties, surely? 'I'm delighted to meet you, Mr Minto,' she said demurely. 'I've never been this close to a tycoon before.'

Amusement glinted in his eyes but he didn't correct her assessment of his standing, only her form of address. 'Keir, please. You must have noticed we're a lot less formal here than you are in England.'

'You know England well?' She was very conscious that he was still holding her hands and that beneath the flow of polite small-talk disturbing currents were running, a galvanising awareness that brought her already stimulated senses to a tight strung pitch.

'As my mother is English, and as I spend two-thirds of my time there, you could say so,' he drawled, and unaccountably Abigail smiled, unaware of how it transformed the rather serious set of her delicate features and lit a glow in her eyes. There was an arrested expression on Keir's face then he too smiled, showing splendidly white even teeth.

'Now you really must come and meet——' The portly little man by her side took her arm firmly to move her on so that Keir was obliged to release her hands. She made a helpless little gesture of regret but he just went on smiling.

For the next half hour, while she listened to congratulations and answered sometimes very personal questions she was aware of him always just in her line of vision, still smiling, the intimacy of his glance each time their eyes met several times making her lose the thread of what she was saying.

And then once when she looked up he had gone. It was as if the source of light and warmth had been abruptly switched off, as if midnight had struck and like Cinderella, all the magic had gone. It was just tiredness of course, she told herself. Up till now the elation of her success had kept the adrenalin pumping through her veins but now that elation had died and she was suffering from reaction. She began to long for the quiet and privacy of her hotel room but still there seemed to be people who were 'just dying' to meet her.

At last their ranks began to thin out, but just when Abigail wearily hoped to make her escape, her pompous host declared, 'I've invited some of the more important people here back to my home for supper, and naturally we hope you'll join us.'

While Abigail was still wondering how she could refuse without mortally offending him a voice said, 'I'm sorry, Edgar, but I've already arranged a very quiet supper for Abigail. Can't you see the poor girl's nearly out on her feet?'

Startled, Abigail looked up into a pair of clear grey eyes that dared her to deny his statement, and while the deflated Edgar was still puffing and protesting a strong arm around her shoulders led her away.

'You look like a startled fawn,' he teased, glancing down at her upturned face.

'I—I thought you'd gone.' And then in case he

should guess how much his disappearance had disappointed her, 'And wasn't that a bit high-handed, leaving that poor man flat like that?'

'You didn't *want* to have supper with him and all those dreary socialites, did you?'

A smile of pure mischief erased the anxiety from her expression as she admitted, 'Well—no! And suddenly I'm not so tired as apparently I look.'

His arm tightened round her shoulders. 'Baby, that wasn't tiredness, that was mind-blowing boredom. And whatever you are for the rest of this night, I promise you won't be bored.'

He opened the door for her and the crisp breeze lifted her hair as a ripple of excitement lifted her heart. A large American-make car stood at the kerb. Keir opened the passenger door and handed her into the seat that sighed as she sank into its luxurious depth.

'I've never seen anything like it!' she gurgled as Keir took his place beside her and switched on the ignition. 'You could get my little Mini in the boot and still have room for luggage.'

'The trunk. In this country we call the boot the trunk.' He took his eyes off the road to glance at her and again Abigail was aware of the turbulent currents beneath this bantering conversation.

He snapped a tape into the stereo deck in the dashboard and Abigail relaxed against the back of her seat as the liquid notes of a Chopin Nocturne washed over her, then moments later she shot upright. 'That's *my* recording!'

'That's right,' he agreed laconically.

'But—but how come? I mean, I didn't think anybody much had ever heard of me yet.'

Again those clear eyes raked her and his mouth curved as he answered, 'Oh, I'd heard of you all right. I've seen you play before too, once at the Purcell Room in London but the first time was at the De Montfort Hall in Leicester.'

'Leicester!' Abigail was astounded. 'What on earth were you doing in *Leicester*?'

'Don't sound so disparaging. I have a house there, or rather on the fringe of a little village about six miles out of the city. It's a good centre, within easy reach of the motorway network yet far enough from London when I want to get away from the hassle.'

'I wasn't being disparaging, I know Leicester well. What's the name of your village?'

'Great Wiston. D'you know it?'

'Know it!' Abigail's voice rose to an incredulous squeak. 'I grew up there! I still go back as often as I can to see my grandmother.'

'Can you beat that!' Keir said softly. 'Maybe you know my house too. It's called Marmion.'

'Oh yes——' She was surrounded by the spangled lights of towering skyscrapers but her mind's eye was seeing the graceful house that had always been a favourite of hers, not so very old, built only at the beginning of the century, and not so very large. But its mellow red brick and stone-mullioned windows gave it a timelessness, set like a jewel against clipped lawns and mature trees and bushes, out of sight of the village, the curving stream that formed the boundary of the garden and divided it from the surrounding lush green fields adding to its dreaming sense of privacy.

'Oh yes, it's a lovely house. Gran told me it had changed hands some time ago but she didn't know who'd bought it.' She shook her head in wonder. 'Isn't that just extraordinary! I come all these thousands of miles to meet a man who lives in the same village as I do.'

'*Lives* in only the very loosest sense,' Keir grimaced. 'I haven't spent much time there so far.' He pulled the car into a parking space. 'Though I'm going to move heaven and earth to be there more often from now on,' he added softly, and the expression in his eyes made the breath catch in Abigail's throat.

Surprisingly in this ultra-modern city, the place Keir had brought her to was a mere three stories high and looked genuinely old, but an even bigger surprise was to find herself eating by soft gaslight. And eating magnificently too on the most delicious seafood she had ever tasted, the first mouthful making her realise how ravenously hungry she was.

Keir watched her, fascinated. 'Where does a little bit of a thing like you put it all? Most women I know never do more than pick at their food.'

It was silly but the reference to the women he knew was like a cold finger touching her. 'Maybe they don't expend as much energy as I do,' she retorted with a touch of asperity. The women he usually associated with must be rich, pampered, certainly wouldn't need to go out and earn their own living. 'Besides,' she admitted candidly, 'All I ate yesterday was the plastic stuff that passes for food on airlines, and as for today—I'm always too keyed up to eat before a concert.'

'Must be a tough life, being a concert pianist,' he commented.

'You certainly need stamina,' she agreed, then grinned. 'But I'm a lot tougher than I look.'

'You'd need to be.' His eyes touched her slender shoulders, bared by the cut of her gown and slid caressingly downwards to the swell of her firm young breasts. 'Do you travel much?'

'I'm beginning to.' She was both relieved and slightly piqued that he had transferred his gaze to his plate. 'I know it means I'm making headway in my career but I can't say I enjoy it much. Flying's boring and living out of a suitcase in one anonymous hotel room after another can be lonely.'

'I know what you mean. Travelling's a necessary evil these days. That's why I like to have a base in the places I visit most, my apartment here in Toronto, the cabin in Manitoba, the apartment in London and of course Marmion. And then there's the ranch in Alberta and the farm in Saskatchewan.' He refilled her glass with a light, locally grown Canadian wine she was beginning to suspect was going to her head.

'You really are a tycoon then?' she asked curiously.

'Well as Edgar Hoyt—the pompous little clown who was squiring you so determinedly this evening—only acknowledges people who can be said to have "arrived", I suppose you could say so.' His grin was engaging and quite without conceit. 'Minto Enterprises is a family concern though, not a one-man band. My father runs the grain-growing side while my sister's husband takes care of the cattle ranch. My brother Andrew handles the mineral extraction and my youngest brother took over Grandfather's lumbering interests. I mostly concentrate on the electronics side myself, hence my need for a base in England.'

'Two brothers and a sister. You come from a big family.' Abigail's unconscious wistful expression betrayed her envy.

'Two brothers and *two* sisters,' he corrected. 'The youngest is still at college. How about you? You have a family?'

Abigail shook her head. 'My parents—my father was a musician too—were killed when I was only a toddler. There's only me and Granny Lucy.'

'The grandmother who brought you up?' His eyes were intent on her face. 'She must miss you when you're gadding about the world.'

'She does. That's why I always go back to Great Wiston when I'm not touring and don't have to be in London.'

'So you come from a musical family. Your grandmother, was she a musician too?'

'A singer. Or rather, she was until she got married.'

'And how about you, Abigail?' He questioned softly. 'Do you have a prospective husband on the horizon?'

His eyes were intent, as if they would see right into

her head, and his question brought a flood of colour to her cheeks. She forced a laugh, shrugging. Why let it embarrass her, a casual question from a casually met stranger? It wasn't as if he was really interested in her answer. 'I never stay in one place long enough to meet any likely candidates.'

'Lovers, then?' he prompted and this time her cheeks scorched.

'The same answer still applies,' she retorted.

The corner of his mouth with the tiny scar quirked upwards. 'You've met me.'

Her dark eyes widened to meet the enigmatic gleam in his. He was teasing, of course, probably believing her to be a lot more experienced at his flirtatious games than in fact she was. 'And tomorrow I move on to Ottawa.' She deliberately kept her voice brisk to cover a stab of regret and was glad when he went on to inquire casually about her tour schedule without betraying a shred of regret himself.

Abigail felt suddenly flat and dispirited as she recited the dates and venues she knew off by heart. 'And now if you don't mind,' she finished, picking up her purse, 'I'd like to go back to my hotel. Thank you for the lovely supper, it was just what I needed to unwind.'

Without a word he signalled the waiter and signed the bill with a flourish before taking her arm and leading her out to the car. The silence stretched as he drove and she attempted a few trite remarks just to break it but he answered only in preoccupied monosyllables so she desisted, wondering if she had offended him. And what if she had? she thought wearily. In just a few minutes they would be saying goodbye and that would be that.

Still without breaking his unnerving silence he slid into a parking space outside her hotel and Abigail turned stiffly to thank him again but he was already climbing out and walking round to open her door. Again she opened her mouth to say her goodbyes but he gave her no chance, slamming the door shut and taking her arm to walk her briskly into the hotel.

'Good evening, Mr Minto,' the night clerk greeted him.

Obviously Keir was known here and Abigail was aware of the man's speculative glance as she gave him her room number, but before she could take her key Keir forestalled her, taking possession of it himself.

'My key! Please give me my key,' she hissed as he steered her towards the lifts, his grip on her arm not relaxing as he urged her inside, making clear his intention of going up with her. 'What will he think!' She cast a backward glance at the night clerk.

'That I'm being the perfect gentleman and seeing you safely to your room, what else?' He sounded amused.

'There's no need,' she protested. 'I'm perfectly capable——'

'There's every need. Even in a hotel like this a girl alone isn't immune from unwelcome attentions.' He pressed the button for her floor and the doors closed.

Unwelcome attentions from whom? Abigail wondered wildly. She kept her head bowed but she was overwhelmingly aware of the burning touch of his hand on her bare arm, of his size and strength, his virile masculinity. Was he expecting 'payment' for taking her out in the form of being invited to share her bed? A shiver that was half fear, half excitement rippled down her spine. If he got into her room would she have the strength to prevent him taking what he wanted? Would she *want* to stop him?

She drew in her breath sharply at the direction of her thoughts. No man had ever impinged on her awareness as this man did but she wasn't the kind of girl to indulge in a one night stand however magnetically attractive he might be, and the sooner she put him straight, the better.

She opened her mouth then closed it again. Suppose she was wrong. Suppose he *was* only being gentlemanly and seeing her to her room. A fine fool she'd look if she accused him of wanting to make love to her when he hadn't as much as kissed her. She twisted the purse in her hands in an agony of indecision, feeling gauche and hopelessly out of her depth.

The lift stopped and Keir steered her out into the silent corridor. They reached her door and he released her arm while he turned the key in the lock, opened the door and reached in to switch on the light. Her heart thumping so loudly she was sure he would hear it, Abigail watched him withdraw the key and hold it out to her.

'I won't come in,' he said, and for the first time since they had got into the lift downstairs she looked up into his face. The dancing amusement in his eyes told her he had read every thought that had passed through her head.

Embarrassment scorched her fair skin and she stiffened her shoulders defensively. Trying to sound coolly formal she held out her hand. 'It's been so nice meeting you, Keir, and thank you for entertaining me.'

He took her hand but instead of shaking it he carried it up to his lips and kissed the finger tips. Her eyes widened and she found she couldn't drag them away from his mouth, even when he lowered her hand.

'Goodnight, Abigail,' he said softly as he released her. 'Sleep well.'

'Goodnight,' she echoed faintly, watching him walk away down the hall.

She closed her bedroom door behind her and leaned against it, fighting a ridiculous sense of disappointment. He'd taken her at her word that there was no future in furthering their acquaintance, and after all those blatant hints of interest in her too, even implying he would spend more time at his home in Great Wiston if it meant being near her. She pushed away from the door, angry with herself for feeling such a sense of loss. He had merely been flirting with her, she told herself,

probably had felt none of the electric awareness that
had devastated her own senses. And anyway, what
alternative could there have been to that casual
'Goodnight'? Her time in Canada was to be short, her
schedule packed, and in two weeks she had to be back
in London for another engagement.

But no matter how sensibly she tried to reason with
herself, she couldn't dispel the sense of flatness. It was
still with her when she arrived in Ottawa, making it
hard to concentrate during rehearsals, disturbing her
when she should have been resting.

Only when she actually sat down at the piano was she
able to put him out of her mind, concentrating fiercely
on the conductor's baton, drowning the insidious
longings for what might have been in her music.

The response to her performance was every bit as
generously enthusiastic as it had been in Toronto but
this time the uplift didn't last. As she walked back to
her dressing room she wished she didn't have to go
through the ritual of the reception in her honour
afterwards. She slumped into the chair in front of the
mirror and stared despondently at her reflection before
automatically repairing her make-up and tidying her
hair.

This was ridiculous! She stiffened her back as a tap
came at the door. She had to snap out of it. She was
behaving like a schoolgirl with a crush, and all over a
man she was never likely to see again.

She called an irritated, 'Come in,' irritated as much
with herself as with this call to duty. But as the door
opened she gave a gasp. The eyes that met hers through
the mirror were no stranger's. 'You!' She whirled round
to face him. 'What on earth are you doing here?'

'Surprised to see me?' Keir's mouth tilted in a
triumphant grin. 'I can't think why. Surely you knew I
didn't intend to let you far out of my sight?'

'Of course I'm surprised. You—you never mentioned
you'd be here at this concert too.' Abigail's heart was

beating fast, her depression miraculously transmuted into a heady excitement.

'After your excruciatingly polite, "it's been nice meeting you" I didn't dare mention it,' he said wickedly. 'Besides——' He drew her to her feet. 'I didn't know if I'd be able to get a ticket at such short notice.'

His closeness and his admission that he'd deliberately pursued her to Ottawa was doing crazy things to her pulse rate. 'Obviously you did.'

'Only after twisting someone's arm. And it took actual bribery to get to be the one to collect you for this bun-fight you unfortunately have to grace.' His hands slid up her arms, his touch vibrating every nerve end, and came to rest on her bare shoulders, his thumbs moving in a circular, sensual caress as they explored the slight hollows beneath her collar bone. His suddenly serious gaze roamed compulsively over her face as if familiarising himself with every feature; the pure oval of her face still with a youthful roundness over her cheekbones, and the delicately chiselled nose, the soft mouth that was perhaps a little too wide for classic beauty but which was vulnerable in its generosity, the brown eyes fringed with a smudge of dark lashes that were so arresting contrasted against the tawny fair mane of hair.

The intensity of his grey eyes as they finally locked with hers brought a self-conscious warmth to her creamy skin. It was almost as if, through the windows of her soul, he could see the turbulence he created inside her, as if he was watching her awareness of herself as a woman stirring into life, as if he was observing her female response to his powerfully male attraction, untried responses that frightened even while they excited her, so far outside her experience were they. She wanted to look away, to hide the newly awakened emotions she didn't know how to control from his all-seeing gaze, but so great was his magnetism she found it impossible.

Her legs trembled. Weakly she raised her hands against his chest in protest but he mistook the gesture. His dark head bent, his firm mouth captured hers in a kiss that was gentle but devastatingly seductive. Time and place ceased to exist and she was lost on an uncharted sea of unimagined sensations; the hard strength of his muscular body, the possessiveness of his hands against her back as he drew her to him, the crispness of his dark hair as her arms slid round his neck, the mind-blowing sensuality of his mouth against hers that made her tremble even as her body yearned for it to go on and on.

'Miss Paston? Mr Minto?' There was an impatient rap on the door.

Keir released her reluctantly and still disorientated Abigail gazed up at him, her eyes wide and dazed. 'Damn this reception,' he swore softly. 'Half an hour and no more. Then I intend to have you all to myself.' He moved to open the door and she was glad of his bulk sheltering her from the eyes of whoever it was had come to fetch them while she regained some composure.

This time Keir refused to surrender her to her host but stayed by her side while she responded to introductions and accepted congratulations on her performance, and true to his word, a little over half an hour later he was extracting her from the gathering and shepherding her to his waiting car.

Which made it all the more surprising when he drove her straight back to her hotel. Abigail's glance flicked up at him and just as quickly flicked away, afraid to let him see her confusion. Dared she tell him she was starving with hunger? she wondered as he steered her towards the lifts. But he hadn't said anything about taking her out to supper, had he? Only that he wanted her all to himself. And as they were going straight up to her room. . . . Her heart thudded like a wild thing in her breast. Had she given him the wrong impression by her response to his kiss? But had it been the wrong impression? Remembering that kiss the same sensations curled through her and she recognised them now as desire.

Panic shot through with excitement brought a light film of moisture to her upper lip. How had she managed to reach the age of twenty-four without learning how to handle a situation like this? Keir wouldn't believe it even if she told him. Knowing she travelled around the world alone so much he would naturally assume she was experienced.

The lift doors opened and her mind still whirling she allowed him to lead her blindly along the carpeted passageway, his hand still enclosing her elbow as he unlocked the door and ushered her inside. But as the door closed behind them she stopped dead, her eyes widening in bewilderment.

'This isn't my room!'

'Of course it isn't!' Keir's mouth curved in amusement. 'You didn't think I was going to let you go to bed hungry, did you? I told you I meant to have you all to myself. I've ordered a meal to be served to us here in my suite.'

'Oh.' For a panicky moment the idea of being alone with him in *his* room was more disconcerting than if it had been her own, but a glance round the large sitting room reassured her. 'I—I didn't realise you were staying in the same hotel.'

'Let me take your coat.' He slid the fake fur jacket off her shoulders and tossed it over a chair. 'Drink?' crossing the room he opened a well-stocked bar, pouring scotch for himself and the martini she asked for.

'I'm not going to fall upon you if you sit down,' he said teasingly as he handed her her glass, and Abigail flushed, subsiding quickly into a chair.

He was about to say something else when a knock at the door heralded a waiter with a heated trolley, and by

the time she was seated at the table she felt much more
at ease.

During the meal Keir talked a lot about himself,
telling her of how, in his vacations from high school
and later from college, he had spent time working in
most of the family enterprises and how, on graduating
with a degree in business studies, he had decided to
move into electronics, believing that to be the industry of
the future.

'You make me feel my life's been very narrow,'
Abigail confessed as they moved to the long sofa to
take their coffee. 'Concentrating solely on music, I
mean.'

'And so you should concentrate on your music when
it gives pleasure to so many people.' His eyes moved
slowly over the deep pink silk jersey gown that clung to
her figure and left her creamy shoulders bare, and his
voice thickened as he went on, 'And just looking at you
gives me pleasure.'

He took her coffee cup from her nerveless fingers,
setting it on the low table in front of them, and drew
her towards him.

'Keir. . . .' Afraid of the strange alchemy of his touch
she tried to protest but as his kisses feathered over her
cheeks, her chin, her nose, her eyes, all protest was
forgotten in the longing for him to take possession of
her lips again, and this time it was her mouth that
sought his.

And this time it was no gentle kiss as he responded to
her seeking mouth. This time he parted her lips with a
passionate hunger that brought the blood roaring in her
ears and ignited licking flames of warmth in her
stomach. He groaned and fell back against the
cushions, dragging her with him, one hand at the nape
of her neck to hold her captive to his searching kiss, the
other moving caressingly over the satin skin of her back
and shoulders.

All doubts, all uncertainties were blotted out of her

mind as she was sucked down into a vortex of
sensation; the feel of his body full length beneath hers,
her breasts crushed against the hard wall of his chest,
the tantalising, arousing touch of his hands, the
pressure of his mouth that was at the same time
drugging and unbearably exciting as it demanded her
surrender, draining all thought of resistance out of her.
And when he finally released her mouth to explore her
neck and the soft swell of her cleavage she gasped
aloud, her breasts tingling in anticipation.

'God, Abigail, I want you so much!' he muttered
hoarsely, and totally inexperienced as she was, she did
not need his words to know of his arousal.

It was when she felt him slide down the zip of her
dress that all the uncertainties and self-consciousness
came rushing back. 'No——' She gave a shudder and
stiffened, pushing away from him.

He let her go at once. 'Pardon me, but I thought I'd
been given the green light,' he said sardonically, sitting up.

Holding the front of her dress against her breasts
with one hand and struggling to do up the zip with the
other, Abigail felt a fool. He watched her struggle
without offering to help. 'There's someone back home
in England, is that it?' His voice was clipped as if he
was trying to contain his anger.

Abigail shook her head. Her dress now safely
fastened she clasped her hands in her lap to stop their
trembling. 'No. I told you, there's never been time to
form any close relationships.'

'Then why?' His voice was suddenly softer. 'I didn't
make a mistake, did I? I did get the green light. So why
the sudden backing off?'

'I—this is the first time I've ever met a man I've
wanted to——' It never occurred to her to prevaricate
but she broke off, her tongue cleaving to the roof of her
mouth in shamed embarrassment. She raised her eyes to
his in unconscious appeal. 'Keir—we don't *know* each
other.'

'And I'm rushing you.' He got up and paced across the room as if the impatience in him demanded the outlet of movement. 'Well I'm not apologising for it,' he said harshly. 'I wanted you the first time I saw you, Abigail.'

Wanted. As if she was some commodity displayed in a shop window he coveted, she thought bleakly, and was stung into the bitter retort, 'And whatever you want, you take.'

His face was stiff, his eyes suddenly cold. 'I think I'd better see you back to your room.'

Silently she picked up her bag and collected her jacket before following him out. Still silently they walked to the lift and when he had taken the key from his pocket to open her door he said a brusque, 'Goodnight,' and walked away.

Undressing, Abigail had to fight back the tears that would keep welling up in her eyes. It was useless to tell herself there had been no future anyway for her and the man who attracted her so much, but the pain of parting from him as enemies hurt unbearably.

The next morning she tried to put all thought of Keir Minto out of her mind and concentrated on the demands the rest of the tour would make on her. But the prospect of the long flight to Vancouver and yet another lonely hotel room depressed her and however hard she tried to think of other things, Keir clung to the edges of her mind with the persistence of a burr.

She breakfasted in her room, eating the maple-syrup drenched waffles she'd ordered even though she had no appetite, but knowing she needed something to sustain her through the long journey. Her heart bounded into her throat at a sharp rap on her door as she was dispiritedly fastening her suitcase but when she answered the summons it was a young man in hotel porter's uniform who said he had been sent to collect her luggage and to tell her a cab was waiting.

Abigail was surprised as she had not got round to

ordering a cab to take her to the airport yet, but put it down to the super-efficiency of the concert tour organiser. Checking that she had left nothing behind she followed the young man out, telling herself she was glad it had not been Keir to disturb her peace of mind again, glad too it was still early and so she would be unlikely to run into him accidentally.

But as she crossed the foyer to deposit her key a tall, all too familiar figure straightened up from the desk. 'Good morning, Abigail.' His eyes took in every detail of the lime green trouser suit she was wearing.

'G-good morning,' she stuttered, her mouth suddenly dry. 'I-I didn't expect to see you again before I left.'

His only answer was a quizzically raised eyebrow as he took her key from her and handed it to the clerk, then one arm lightly round her shoulders he turned her away from the desk.

'I-I'm afraid I'm leaving now,' she said breathlessly. 'My cab's already waiting.'

'I know. I ordered it,' he drawled.

'You did!' She was so astonished she stumbled and his arm tightened to steady her.

'Well we have a plane to catch, don't we? To Vancouver?'

Abigail stopped dead in her tracks. 'We?' she said faintly, staring at him.

'That's right.' As oblivious to his surroundings as if they were the only occupants of the busy hotel lobby Keir brushed a straying strand of fair hair off her cheek and tucked it tenderly behind her ear. 'I'm coming with you.'

CHAPTER THREE

VANCOUVER was like nothing Abigail had ever imagined. From her high hotel bedroom window she could see many other skyscraper blocks but there was a liberal sprinkling of people-sized buildings in between, and plenty of green to ease the eye. Beyond a stretch of water she could see pine-clad forest slopes and beyond that more water and more city against a backdrop of snow-capped mountains. It was very early, with little stirring that she could see, and the sky was a pale washed blue until it met the banks of white cloud over the mountain tops.

This time yesterday, Abigail reflected, she had felt unutterably depressed, but today it was as if champagne ran in her veins. Yesterday Keir's announcement that he was flying to Vancouver with her had stunned her into gaping silence. It wasn't until they had checked in their baggage at the airport that she really believed he meant it and she managed to stutter incoherently,

'B . . . but why, Keir? I mean, last night I thought—well you couldn't wait to get rid of me, could you, when——'

'When I didn't get what I wanted?' he broke in ruefully. 'I guess I did behave like a kid who'd had his candy bar snatched away and I'm sorry. You had every right to turn me down if that was how you felt about it and it was unforgivable of me to take out my frustration on you.'

'I—I don't suppose it's happened to you before, a woman turning you down, I mean?' There was a hollow feeling where her stomach ought to be at the thought of other women lying in his arms, women far less prudish than herself, responding to his kisses and caresses without inhibition.

A faint flush suffused the skin over his cheekbones and Abigail was astonished to see he looked disconcerted. 'I've never met a girl who says exactly what she thinks before, without the usual female coyness and double talk. But to answer your question——' his voice hardened. 'No, it hasn't happened before, not since my youth anyway. And there's no need to look so damned disapproving. What's wrong with a man and a woman making love if they find each other mutually attractive?'

Abigail wished she hadn't got herself into this argument. Keir was the experienced one after all. She couldn't speak with any first-hand knowledge herself. She shrugged, muttering, 'Nothing I suppose, if that's what they both want. Though——' she tacked on, unable to hide her true feelings even if he did laugh at her naivety, '——doesn't that turn what should be a very special relationship into something trivial and meaningless?'

But Keir didn't laugh. His eyes were deadly serious as he looked into her troubled face. 'I don't think what there is between us could ever be trivial and meaningless, Abby.' He took her hands, bringing them close to his chest. 'I still want you, more than I've ever wanted any woman, but I promise you there'll be no more displays of temper. I'll do my best to contain my impatience until *you* want it too. And you will.'

Gazing now on the panorama of city, forest, water and mountains spread out before her Abigail was shaken by a tremor that was half apprehension, half unbearable excitement as she remembered the conviction in Keir's voice, the deadly seriousness of his gaze. Nervous apprehension was something she was accustomed to; it afflicted her every time she awaited her cue to walk out on to a concert platform. But this coruscating excitement was entirely new and she couldn't quite understand herself.

Keir had made no secret of the fact that he had accompanied her to Vancouver with only one idea in mind, to persuade her to succumb to his attractions and invite him into her bed. Did she want that kind of short-lived affair? Abigail was almost certain that she didn't. Something deep inside her recoiled from the idea, that she should be just another of Keir's casual conquests. It undermined her sense of identity, her conception of herself as a unique human being, and something in the new emotions Keir had awoken within her revolted against it.

And yet the thought of spending a whole day in his company filled her with elation. Yesterday there had been the long flight, the chasing up of her contacts to verify the arrangements for the concert and tomorrow she would be embroiled in rehearsals. But today she would explore Vancouver with Keir. As she trod across the carpet to the bathroom she had never felt more vibrantly alive.

Shampooing her hair under the shower, Abigail then wrapped herself sarong fashion in a large towel and sat down at the dressing table with a small hand dryer, lifting the heavy, tawny fair tresses away from her head and shaping the ends with a brush. It was long and very thick so it was almost time to meet Keir in the coffee shop for breakfast before it was dry, leaving her little time to worry unduly over her appearance even if she'd wanted to. And today she was in holiday mood. Today she didn't have to worry about being in the public eye and could be herself.

Hurriedly dragging on a pair of close-fitting jeans and a skinny t-shirt she tied her hair back with a ribbon and with a smudge of eyeshadow and a slick of lip gloss over her full mouth, she was ready.

Eager anticipation was in her face and in the graceful swing of her body as she walked with a light step into the coffee shop. Keir was already there looking overwhelmingly attractive in pearl grey pants, casual but beautifully cut, with a matching silk knit shirt open at the tanned column of his throat. He stood as she approached, his clear eyes sparkling appreciatively as they slid over her curves.

'What happened to you?' He held her chair and her heart beat erratically at his nearness as she sat down.

'Am I late? I'm sorry,' she apologised as he resumed his seat.

He looked at the thin gold watch on his wrist. 'No, you're remarkably punctual. I meant where's the cool, self-assured concert pianist of yesterday? This morning you look about fifteen.'

Abigail certainly didn't *feel* fifteen, not with her senses vibrating wildly in response to this man's effortless charisma, but if her appearance embarrassed him. . . . She sighed. 'I suppose it was the unexpected chance of playing hooky—no practising, no rehearsal, no performance—a day out of time.' There was an unconscious wistfulness in her voice; there had been few such irresponsible days in her dedicated life. She smiled at him reassuringly across the table. 'Don't worry, I'll change into something more suitable after breakfast.'

Her hand, nervously toying with a fork, was suddenly stilled by the pressure of Keir's much larger one. 'Hey, you surely didn't think I was complaining! You look good enough to eat. But I guess——' he glanced wryly at the waitress coming to collect their order, '——I'll just have to make do with an ordinary breakfast—for now,' he added with a look that sent her pulses leaping.

'So what would you like to do with your "day out of time"?' Keir asked as they were finishing their last cups of coffee. 'I guess Granville Street is a "must", where all the big stores are.'

'That would be nice,' Abigail murmured politely, but her unguarded expression revealed her disappointment.

Keir leaned back in his chair, his eyes narrowing. 'Now why do I get the feeling that idea doesn't appeal to you?'

'I'm sorry.' Embarrassed colour reddened her cheeks. 'I'm sure the Vancouver stores must be worth seeing, and if you have some shopping to do, of course I'll be happy to come along. I suppose coming on this trip on the spur of the moment——'

'There's nothing *I* need, but I've yet to meet a woman who could resist a shopping spree——' the little scar above his lip emphasised the cynical curl of his mouth '——especially when she's with a man she knows can buy her anything her fancy lights on.'

Abigail gasped. Shock at his contemptuous disparagement of women and something like a pitying curiosity as to the reason behind this contempt were quickly dispelled by a furious anger that he should see her as self-seeking as the women he was obviously used to consorting with.

'Is that why you think I agreed to spend the day with you? For what I could get out of it? No man buys my favours, Mr Minto. And now if you don't mind, I'll spend the day as *I* want—and alone.' Her fingers clenched round her bag she pushed back her chair and stalked out of the coffee shop, her back rigid with outrage.

Her first instinct was to retreat to her room but when her furious eyes lit on the book shop that was part of the hotel complex she dived inside. If she was to retrieve anything of this day that had promised so well but that had turned out so disastrously, she would need a guide book. But her eyes were swimming with tears and it was difficult to see anything, so she was grateful when an assistant asked if she could help and pointed out the stand.

Abigail dashed the tears away with the back of her hand before she reached to take one of the books down. Her arm was still raised when a hand descended on her shoulder and a warm voice full of contrition said, 'Abigail, I've offended you and I'm sorry.'

Even while her mind rejected his apology her body

shuddered in response to his touch and she was ashamed of her weakness. Afraid to turn round to face him she said coldly, 'Might I remind you I didn't *ask* you to come to Vancouver with me, and I certainly didn't ask to be humiliated.'

His grip on her shoulder tightened. 'Believe me there was no humiliation intended and I can only beg your forgiveness.' He groaned. 'I'll admit experience has disillusioned me where female motives are concerned, but I should have known you were different.'

She was no match for his greater physical strength as he turned her to face him but she refused to lift her eyes farther than the buttons of his shirt. 'I don't see why you should,' she said bleakly, wishing she had more experience to draw on to tell her how to handle this man and his insidious attraction. 'We are still strangers after all, and likely to remain so.'

Keir tilted her chin, forcing her to look at him, inwardly cursing his crass clumsiness for putting the hurt in her eyes and raising this barrier between them. The contradictory mixture of physical fragility and inner strength, of naive youthfulness and cool self-possession, of innocence and passion intrigued him as nothing had ever done before and the desire to unravel the complexities of this lovely girl was becoming an obsession.

'Strangers?' he jeered softly. 'You know that isn't true. We were never strangers. Right from the first moment there's been something between us so don't try to deny it. I don't know what it is yet, but——'

'Physical attraction,' Abigail broke in quickly before the intentness of his grey eyes, the warmth and strength of his touch could crumble any more of her puny defences. 'It can't be anything new to you, even if it is to me.'

'And you think that's why I followed you to Ottawa and muscled in on this trip out West?' he said softly. 'Because I lusted after you?'

'Haven't you already admitted it?' She could recall his actual words. 'I can't imagine you would have followed me all the way here to Vancouver if you'd got what you wanted that night in Ottawa.'

She expected anger at her jibe but was thrown off-balance when his mouth curved into a mocking smile and his eyes slid over her slender figure so blatantly it was almost a physical caress. 'Don't undersell yourself, darling. I have a notion your delectable body would be very difficult to forget. In fact it could light a flame only more of the same could satisfy. And more. . . .'

'Keir!' He had spoken softly, and tucked away as they were behind the travel-guide stand it was unlikely anyone had overheard, but the intimacy of both his words and his tone set her eyes darting about in nervous embarrassment as her face reddened.

He laughed delightedly at her confusion. 'So, if the fleshpots of the city stores hold no appeal, what *would* you like to do with your day?'

Abigail stepped back a pace, trying to control her erratic pulse and build her defences again. 'I was about to buy a guide to find out,' she said stiffly. 'I need to know where to find the places of special interest, the sights I ought to see.'

'All right, you want to go sightseeing, but you won't need that.' Effortlessly he took the guide she was still clutching and replaced it on the rack. 'I know Vancouver well so let's forget this nonsense about seeing it on your own. Come on, I've got a hire-car waiting.'

Allowing no protest he swept her out of the bookshop, across the foyer and out to the parking lot. 'We'll begin on a high note with one of the most spectacular sights,' he said when he had handed her into her seat and was easing the car into the flow of traffic.

Abigail knew some response was expected of her but she refused to give it, deliberately nursing her resentment at his high-handedness.

'Capilano Suspension Bridge,' Keir said, just as if she *had* asked the expected question, and somehow his bland determination to ignore her sulks brought a reluctant tug of amusement to her mouth.

But it was when they reached an intersection and she saw the intriguing name Lost Lagoon Drive that her resistance finally melted and she commented on it.

'The Lost Lagoon is a bird reserve now,' Keir told her as she looked back at the lake dotted with small islands. 'Years ago the water used to drain away at low tide so that's how it got its name. Actually all this is part of Stanley Park, the whole peninsula, a thousand acres in all, of which eight hundred are still in their natural state.'

'It's certainly beautiful,' Abigail conceded, relaxing back in her seat to enjoy the scenery.

Before long they were passing over a bridge that Keir informed her was called Lion's Gate and only a short time later he was drawing on to the parking lot in the Capilano Bridge grounds.

To Abigail's eyes the suspension bridge looked impossibly fragile, stretching high above the Capilano River Canyon, and her grip on Keir's hand tightened nervously as it seemed to move beneath her feet. They paused in the middle and though the view was breathtaking, Abigail closed her eyes. With the river far below—two hundred and thirty feet according to Keir—and the sensation of nothing solid beneath her feet, it made her feel dizzy.

'Nervous?' Keir teased, and pulled her against him.

Leaning back against the solidly muscled length of his body Abigail was able to open her eyes again. 'It's a bit like flying without an airplane.'

'Or hang-gliding without actually making the jump,' he capped.

Abigail was beginning to get used to the motion of the bridge beneath her feet by the time they left it and she felt exhilarated. As they walked back to the car she pointed at a large building. 'What's that?'

'You wouldn't be interested in that,' Keir said wickedly. 'It's a store specialising in local products; furs, totem poles, Cowichan Indian sweaters, jade jewellery. . . .'

'No, of course not.' She turned her head away to hide her suddenly warm cheeks at this reminder of her vehement repudiation of an interest in shopping. Actually she *would* have liked to browse round this place, perhaps buy a souvenir of the trip, and she had the uneasy suspicion that Keir was well aware of this.

Maybe she had over-reacted to Keir's cynical remark at breakfast, she thought uncomfortably. She had only needed to tell him firmly that shops were only shops whatever city in the world it happened to be, and that she had no intention of allowing him to spend money on her, instead of making a big issue of it. But she felt she couldn't back down now, and quickened her footsteps towards the car.

Keir turned north again and after about a mile he pointed out the Capilano salmon hatchery, but they didn't stop until they reached the foot of Grouse Mountain and the Cleveland Dam where the river flowed into Capilano Lake.

'It's a great skiing centre in winter,' Keir told her, 'just half an hour from downtown. But it's well worth a visit in summer too.'

They were just in time to catch the hundred seater Superskyride cable car without a wait and Abigail was all eyes on the breathtaking ride to the top of the mountain, unaware that Keir was watching her expressive face rather than the passing scenery.

His arm around her shoulders had a new protectiveness as they alighted and he led her to what he told her was his favourite vantage point. And Abigail could easily see why. Spread out four thousand feet below them was the city of Vancouver set in a panorama of blue water dotted with green islands and backed by misty topped mountains.

'Look.' Standing behind her, turning her slightly, his head very close to hers and one arm over her shoulder to lead her eyes in the right direction, Keir pointed into the far distance. 'Can you see? It's not very clear today but that's Mount Rainier in Washington State, USA.'

Abigail strained her eyes and thought she could make it out, but she was too conscious of his breath on her cheek, his warm body against her back.

'It's a pity we don't have time to explore some of the trails up here,' Keir said as they sipped a restoring cup of coffee and rested their feet. 'But as you've set an ambitious programme I guess we'd better move on.'

This time he turned the car south, driving back the way they had come but after they'd crossed Lion's Gate Bridge back into Stanley Park, Abigail said excitedly, 'Oh look, there's a zoo!'

'You want to go to the zoo?' Keir's eyebrows rose incredulously.

'Oh please, Keir,' Abigail's eyes sparkled. 'I've never been to one before.'

'So be it!' he said resignedly.

It wasn't a big zoo and there were no exotic animals, and though Abigail couldn't help feeling the polar bears were rather pathetic out of their natural environment, their coats a yellowish colour instead of the pure white she'd expected, she was delighted with the penguins who seemed quite happily at home in their pool, and couldn't help but admire the speed and grace of the sea otters in the water. But it was the amusing antics of the monkeys that kept her attention the longest, particularly the ministrations of a mother monkey to the baby she held in her arms just like any human mother.

'This is a side of you I never imagined,' Keir said softly, watching her almost childlike fascination. 'Why do I get the feeling you missed out on being a child?'

Startled out of her absorption Abigail looked up at him. 'Missed out? Oh no, I don't think so.' Her childhood had been happy, Granny Lucy had seen to that. And yet from a very early age her music had left little room for sharing the pastimes of her contemporaries at the village school, and later still, when she had been away at school, music had absorbed all the more of her time and interest.

'Well, perhaps, in a way,' she conceded. 'It stretched Granny Lucy's resources to send me to a special school for musically gifted children even though the local education authority helped, so there was never much to spare for this kind of expedition during the holidays. I certainly never considered I missed out on anything though. I used to play down at the recreation ground with the other children—though I always had to be careful of my hands—and I remember the fun-fair coming to the village a few times.'

'No swimming in rivers? No climbing trees and riding ponies?' He looked at her quizzically.

'No.' She grinned at him. 'I don't think I was ever a tomboy. Is that what you did?' Somehow she could see him, a sturdy, dark-haired, serious-eyed little boy, as determined to get his own way then as he was now.

'And some! What with brothers and sisters and the children of the ranch hands there was always a bunch of us looking for mischief. Hey, I know what you would enjoy.' He grasped her hand and hurried her over to a kiosk where he purchased two tickets for the miniature train ride, and seemed to get as much enjoyment out of the juvenile amusement as Abigail did.

But Keir's sophisticated tastes reasserted themselves when it came to giving her lunch. Scorning the Stanley Park Pavilion where most people seemed to be making for, he drove her to Beach Avenue where they lunched on the terrace of an elegant establishment overlooking the blue waters of English Bay.

After that it was back to the car and a lightning tour of the city itself, circling the West End where he pointed out the Nitobe Japanese Garden and the University of

British Columbia then cutting across town so she could at least *see* the fashionable stores he had thought she would hanker after before making for the Heritage Village Museum, a recreation of history showing the way of life in the Lower Mainland from 1890, complete with staff in period costume.

'Are you bushed or are you game for more?' Keir asked when they had covered every inch of the place and seen everything there was to see.

Abigail's feet were aching and she *was* tired, but somehow the day that had started so badly had taken on a magical quality. She had discovered Keir's sense of humour wasn't always mocking and that it often chimed in with her own, that he could be an entertaining companion who demanded nothing of her except that she be her natural self. He had withdrawn the blatantly sexual challenge that confused and disturbed her so much, though she was still very much aware of his magnetic attraction. But this she could handle. It made her feel very much alive.

'I'm game,' she said firmly, reluctant for this 'day out of time' to end.

The big car surged forward, soon reaching the waterfront and following it so Abigail could see the craft on the water. 'I know I promised to keep you away from the shops, Keir said with a gleam of his former mockery, 'but Gastown you must see.'

And when they reached it, Abigail understood why. It was an area of great charm, a small urban village of squares, cobbled mews and courtyards.

'You'd never believe this was once the city's Skid Row, would you?' Keir said as they wandered in and out of cul-de-sacs gazing into antique shops, boutiques and art galleries.

'Just as you'd never believe Covent Garden was once a noisy, smelly fruit and vegetable market to see it now,' Abigail laughed, a street musician playing to the shoppers in Maple Tree Square reminding her of home.

'Oh, I love that knitwear!' She pointed to a display in a shop window.

'They're the Cowichan Indian sweaters I was telling you about.' Keir moved towards the shop doorway. 'Like to try one on?'

Abigail hesitated. She *did* fancy one. They looked warm and cosy enough to combat any English winter, chunky in raw, undyed wool. 'Yes, but I shall buy it for myself,' she said, lifting her chin.

Keir made no protest as she paid out her dollars, nor later when she bought a polar bear carved out of soapstone to take home for her grandmother, but when she paused at another window to look at a display of jade he said, 'I don't suppose you'll allow me to buy you one of those trinkets?'

For just a moment, remembering his cynical view that inside every woman was a gold digger, she fizzed with temper. But this time she was determined not to over-react and controlling her anger she said coolly, 'You suppose right,' and turned away from the shop.

'Pity.' He caught one of her parcels as it slid from beneath her arm and she couldn't help glancing up at him curiously.

'I don't understand you. If you dislike giving presents to your women friends so much then why do you do it?'

'Who said I disliked it?'

A puzzled frown creased her brow as she looked up into his enigmatic face. 'Well from your remark this morning you seem to get precious little pleasure from it. You obviously despise women for accepting your gifts. Or is that it?' Her dark eyes widened. 'Do you like buying them things so you have an excuse to despise them?'

His face darkened and his grey eyes glittered with such an icy anger that Abigail was afraid she'd gone too far. 'You think that was what I was trying to do just now?' he said tightly. 'Buy you a trinket so I could have an excuse to despise you?'

Abigail's face flooded with colour and then just as quickly it all drained away leaving a transparent pallor. 'I—I don't know,' she muttered.

'Contrary to what your naive little mind seems to think, there are plenty of women more interested in the bank balance than the man,' he ground out.

Unable to help herself she glanced up at his face, still undeniably attractive in spite of his glowering anger, and burst out involuntarily, 'I find that hard to believe!'

To her utter astonishment his face was wiped clean of anger as he threw back his head and bellowed with laughter. 'Oh Abigail! Honest even into the jaws of death! Thank you at least for that.'

Would she ever understand this man? she wondered as they drove back to the hotel.

She was still wondering the same much later that night when he merely kissed her goodnight and pushed her into her room. True, she had almost fallen asleep over her dinner after all the fresh air and exercise during the day but knowing Keir's determination to persuade her into his bed she had expected him to take advantage of her lowered defences to make another assault on her senses instead of gently putting her away from him.

When she went down to the coffee shop the next morning it was to find Keir had already breakfasted and gone. She couldn't help but feel piqued but there was little time to puzzle over his tactics. At ten o'clock the car arrived to take her to the concert hall to meet the conductor and to begin rehearsals, and all her concentration was centred on her work.

It wasn't until she was resting in the afternoon trying to subdue pre-performance nerves that she allowed herself to wonder what Keir had done with his day. Perhaps after their last quarrel that had ended so improbably with his laughter he had given up on her. Perhaps that early, solitary breakfast meant that he had cut his losses and gone back to Toronto. Abigail tried to tell herself that if he had, it was all for the best. The last thing she needed at this stage in her career was any emotional entanglement, not even the casual, fleeting affair that was all Keir was interested in. But that he should have left without a word, without saying goodbye—it hurt much more than it should have done.

Trying to blank out her mind to that hurt she thought instead of certain suggestions the conductor had made at rehearsals concerning the piece she was playing that night. But as she showered and dressed in the uncrushable rose gown that was so useful on these trips where she was living out of a suitcase, Keir's image kept intruding.

The day in the sunshine had put a touch of honey into her creamy complexion. Abigail studied her reflection after she had swept the sides of her long fair hair up on to the crown of her head and fastened them in place with a comb that matched her dress. Self-possessed, Keir had said of her public image, and she supposed he was right. Little of the churning nerves that dried her mouth showed on the surface.

But that self-possession was shattered a few moments later when, after a peremptory knock the door of her room opened and she whirled round to see Keir standing there. It was almost as if the power of her thoughts had conjured him up and she stared at him mutely, her face draining of colour.

He crossed the room quickly, taking her hands and looking down at her in concern. 'Abby, are you all right?'

'Yes.' She licked her lips and found her voice. 'Yes, I'm fine. You startled me, that's all.'

'I'm sorry, I didn't think. I suppose you do get jumpy before a concert.' His hands moved lightly, reassuringly against her bare shoulders. 'Ready?' And when she stared at him blankly, 'I'm taking you to the concert hall,' he said gently.

'What have you been doing with yourself all day?'

The need to know forced the question out of her when she was seated beside him in the car.

'Working, what else?' His wryly smiling glance noted her eyebrows rising in surprise. 'Minto Enterprises has an office here in Vancouver,' he explained. 'There was a lot to catch up on after neglecting things for several days.'

Abigail felt a stab of compunction that it was on her account he was neglecting his business but it did nothing to diminish the blazing happiness that gripped her. Keir hadn't gone back to Toronto after all, and neither had he been amusing himself with one of his women friends. She didn't question the reasons for her unaccountable joy but it spilled out in her music and echoes of it were felt by every member of the audience that night.

Again Keir stayed close by her side at the reception afterwards and again he spirited her away for a quiet supper when he felt she had had enough. The shining happiness stayed with her until Keir was escorting her back to her room when suddenly it faltered, draining away into uncertainty.

Tonight was her last night in Vancouver. Tomorrow she had to move on to Calgary for her next engagement. Tonight Keir would expect—— She found she was trembling uncontrollably. Half of her wanted so much to know his kisses and caresses again, to surrender to his overwhelming male magnetism, but the other half, the sane half, froze in rejection, the knowledge deep inside her that one night wouldn't be enough, that once she let this man possess her she would thirst for him forever.

Keir unlocked the door and pushed it open. While every nerve in her body clamoured to melt into his arms she held herself rigidly.

'I suppose this time will have to be goodbye, Keir.' Her voice even to her own ears sounded unreal, controlled, oddly precise. 'I leave Vancouver first thing in the morning.'

Keir looked through the open door of her room and then back at Abigail's strained face. 'I take it you're not ready to invite me in yet?'

She shook her head. 'No. Please Keir, don't——' There was a note of desperation in her voice because she was not at all sure she would be able to hold out against his persuasion, but he stopped her mouth with two gentle fingers laid across her lips.

'Then I'll just have to follow you on to Calgary, won't I?' he said calmly.

Keir hadn't been joking. And after Calgary he followed her on to Edmonton, making sure they spent as much time together as possible, keeping her ever more acutely aware of him and yet not pushing her. It was as if he was so confident of her final capitulation he was content to wait for it, and sometimes Abigail found this almost frightening, because she was nowhere near as confident of her ability to stand out against him.

So it was crazy to feel so wildly, unreasoningly happy to be with him, to feel such sharp delight in his company. She told herself it was because nothing like this had ever happened to her before. While she had been a student there had been mild flirtations but no man had ever pursued her with such determination, and that it should be happening to her now and with such a man as Keir was flattering to her ego, elating to her senses. Keir was a very attractive man, his experience with women giving him a devastating technique at arousing female response. He was man, the hunter, enjoying the chase, but would he find the final capitulation of his quarry as exciting as the ancitipation? Knowing herself to be entirely ignorant of how to please a man, Abigail very much doubted it. Surely that knowledge was enough to make sure she didn't lose her head?

Another aspect of Keir's pursuit made her uneasy too. She knew he must be neglecting his business in order to follow her around Canada and she couldn't help wondering if his business colleagues and employees knew the reason for that neglect.

It was in Regina that this unease crystallised. When Abigail joined Keir at breakfast the morning after her recital there she found him frowning over a newspaper, so absorbed he was unaware of her approach.

'What's the matter? Have your share prices taken a dive?' she teased as she sat down.

Keir looked up visibly startled and made a move as if about to hide what he'd been reading, then apparently changing his mind he folded the paper so the relevant item was uppermost and handed it to her. 'I'm very much afraid we've made the gossip columns,' he said wryly.

Abigail's eyes widened as she looked at the photographs, one of herself—a publicity handout—and one of Keir, obviously taken at some business function. Beneath the photographs was a caption, *A new romance for business tycoon?*

With a hollow feeling of disbelief she read that the well-known businessman Keir Minto, Canada's most eligible bachelor, had been devotedly following Abigail Paston the young English pianist around the country on her concert tour. It facetiously went on to suggest that although Mr Minto had long been a music lover, wasn't there perhaps more than a love of *music* behind this devotion? Mr Minto had attended every concert on her tour so far and had hardly left the beautiful Miss Paston's side, travelling with her and staying in the same hotels. It then listed a number of ladies who had enjoyed Mr Minto's company in the past and implied these same ladies were now eating their hearts out since the advent of the lovely Miss Paston in the playboy businessman's life.

Abigail's face burned. She had forgotten Keir was a well-known figure, at least in his own country, and that his actions might arouse interest and comment.

'Don't look so appalled,' Keir said in a bored voice.

'You must surely be used to seeing your name in the papers by now.'

'In the critical columns, yes, but never like this. They've made it sound——' She choked, crumpling the humiliating article out of sight.

'—As if we're having an affair,' he finished for her. 'They haven't actually said so.'

'No, but it's what everyone will believe.' Abigail darted a glance around the room. Everyone else seemed to be breakfasting unconcernedly but she felt rawly exposed, the object of speculation and knowing sniggers. 'Even if what they're implying *was* true, I don't care to have my private life offered up as a tit-bit on all and sundry's breakfast table.'

'Cool down, Abby. Even the readers of that rag must realise that what these scandalmongers don't know they make up. It's certainly not worth getting uptight about.'

He sounded enviably calm and matter of fact but Abigail was unable to take it so philosophically. 'Don't you *mind* the gutter press intruding on your life like this?'

He shrugged and his voice was distant as he said, 'I've learned to live with it. Unfortunately I can see you haven't.'

And he blamed her for that? Saw her as over-sensitive and prudish? 'No, and I can't imagine ever growing a skin thick enough to shrug it off like you,' she said quietly. 'But then I suppose this sort of thing only enhances a *man's* reputation.'

A muscle twitched along his jaw and a momentary gleam of savagery in his eyes told her he was not quite as sanguine about it as he pretended. 'All right, I'm sorry I've dragged the purity of your reputation down to my level,' he ground out. 'But what do you expect me to do about it? If I make a fuss and issue a denial it's going to cause even more talk.'

The waitress coming for their order gave Abigail time to think. Keir was right, of course. A response to the innuendoes in the scandal sheet would probably only make matters worse.

'There is a way to give the lie to the rumour,' she said slowly after the waitress had departed, and Keir raised an interrogative eyebrow as he poured her coffee. 'You could leave me to finish the rest of my tour on my own.'

'No!' His mouth tightened angrily as he put the coffee pot down.

Abigail gripped her hands together to still their trembling. 'Keir,' she pleaded, 'it's been bothering me that you must've been neglecting your business to follow me around as you have. Can't you see that that alone was bound to cause speculation?'

'No!' he repeated vehemently. 'Abigail, I'm damned if I'll let any tattlemonger break up what there is between us.'

But what *was* there between them to break up? Abigail wondered bleakly. A powerful sexual attraction, yes, but certainly on Keir's part it was no more than that. He'd made it plain he wanted her, but he'd also made it plain he was not looking for any kind of commitment. His lack of concern at having made her the target of gossip columnists proved how little he really cared for her, how little her feelings mattered to him. The knowledge was unexpectedly painful, tearing at her with sharp, jagged claws.

She pushed her plate away untasted and sat up straight in her chair, assuming an unconscious dignity that, had she known it, had a greater effect on the man sitting opposite than any display of temper might have done.

'Keir, I still have two concerts of my tour to complete. Tomorrow night in Winnipeg and again for my final concert in Toronto I have to get up on that platform and face an audience. Don't you think it's hard enough knowing my musical ability is being judged each time I appear without the added burden of knowing my morals are being judged and speculated about too?'

Something flickered in Keir's eyes but was gone before Abigail could identify it and the shutters came down over his expression. Only the little scar on his upper lip gave a touch of cynicism as he said, 'And you think you're tough enough to handle the speculation on your own?'

Abigail quailed inwardly but refused to allow her apprehension to show. 'If you're not there to confirm the rumours, I think I can handle it,' she claimed.

Keir shrugged. 'If that's the way you want it. Maybe I should check out things at the ranch while I'm in this part of the country.'

His sudden indifference after his earlier vehement refusal to let her go on alone was somehow shocking and Abigail flinched visibly. But Keir was already pushing back his chair and standing up.

He was going! She moistened her dry lips. 'Maybe—maybe we could meet up in Toronto to say goodbye,' she found herself suggesting, and then wished she hadn't as his coldly mocking glance pinned her to her chair.

'Suddenly so brave, Abigail?'

It was what you wanted, wasn't it? she asked herself fiercely as she watched him walk away. But deep down she knew it wasn't. Keir Minto had had a profound effect on her from the first moment they met but it wasn't until now, seeing him walk out of her life for good, that she admitted to herself just how far-reaching and ineradicable that effect had been.

He had made her fall in love with him. Improbable, impossible, crazy even, that he could have awakened such a depth of feeling in such a short time. And yet what had time to do with it? Hadn't there been that flash of recognition that first night in Toronto, that sense of inevitability? And then there had been the amazing coincidence of Keir being the new owner of

Marmion, the lovely house so near to her grandmother's home in Great Wiston?

Abigail blinked back the tears that filmed her eyes. She had forgotten that in the heady excitement of Keir's pursuit of her across Canada, forgotten too his remark when they had made the discovery that they both had a base in the same English village that he would have to make sure he spent more time there in future. A flicker of hope stirred a flame to life in the ashes of her despair. Perhaps he hadn't gone out of her life for good after all. Surely there was a chance they would meet again? Great Wiston was a small place.

But the cold wind of reality blew out that flame as she remembered Keir's indifference, his cold mockery. The flash of recognition that had changed her life had left Keir untouched. The only sense of inevitability he had recognised was that her response to his lovemaking must inevitably lead her to his bed. He had expected an easy conquest but it hadn't happened and that had hurt his pride. He had wanted her but he hadn't wanted her love, and he never would.

CHAPTER FOUR

STIFFLY Abigail got up from the table and took the lift to her room. Like an automaton she packed her clothes and asking the receptionist to call her a cab to take her to the airport, she checked out of the hotel.

The cloudless blue sky arched above the aircraft and down below were spread the golds and browns of the prairies but Abigail's eyes saw nothing of them. The sun might be shining but she was locked inside a grey world that seemed to stretch bleakly into the foreseeable future.

In Winnipeg she had to retrieve her own luggage, find her own cab to take her to the hotel where the tour organiser had booked her a room. She had to dine alone, and the following morning breakfast alone before finding her way to the concert hall to try out the piano.

She told herself nothing had changed. She had done all this before in most of the principal cities of Europe and many of the lesser ones, and it had always been lonely. But now a new dimension had been added to her loneliness, the memory of companionship and shared laughter, the ache for what might have been if only Keir had returned her feelings, and she knew nothing would ever be the same again.

In spite of the extra hard practice at the piano with which Abigail filled the lonely hours she knew her recital in Winnipeg that night, though technically faultless, lacked the sparkle, the joyous spontaneity of her earlier Canadian concerts. She was unaware that the depth of feeling she put into the sad little Chopin Nocturne she elected to play as an encore left hardly a dry eye in the auditorium.

The future seemed even more bleak and empty as she flew back to Toronto, but even so she couldn't help her eyes searching the throng at the busy airport for Keir's commanding height, his lean, dark arrogance. Of course he wasn't there. Cold with misery in spite of the heat she found a cab and booked into the hotel where she had stayed on her first visit, spending the rest of the day lying on her bed staring up at the ceiling.

At least she had the rehearsal the following morning to take her mind off her aching unhappiness, and afterwards, not wanting any lunch, she stayed on to use the piano for some private practice, driving herself hard, sublimating the passion Keir had wakened in her into her music. A couple of hours drained her into a kind of numbness and tiredly she returned to the hotel to rest.

She had a tray of coffee sent up to her room and after drinking a couple of cups she undressed and stepped under the shower, hoping the warm needles would slough off some of her tension. She was drying herself on the big fluffy towel when the knock came at her bedroom door. Slipping into a thin black silk robe and tying it tightly round her narrow waist she picked up the coffee tray as she crossed the room and opened the door to hand it to the floor waiter.

But it was no white-coated floor waiter who stood there. 'Hallo, Abby,' Keir said, and her hands shook so much the crockery jangled.

He took the tray from her and bent to put it on the floor of the corridor outside her room then came in, closing the door behind him. 'It's all right,' he said quietly. 'I used the elevator from the parking bay so no one saw me come up.'

Abigail stared at him, her eyes hungrily taking in the width of his shoulders beneath the linen shirt he wore, the tanned column of his throat, the dark vitality of his hair, the level brows, the strong planes of his cheekbones and jaw, the little scar on his upper lip that this time gave his mouth a look of rare diffidence instead of cynicism. And in that moment she wouldn't have cared if he'd announced his arrival with a fanfare of trumpets. Keir had come back!

'I—I didn't think I'd see you again,' she whispered.

'I didn't think you'd want to.' He stood just inside the door, unmoving, his expression guarded.

Her heart thudded and the tip of her tongue moistened her lips. She swayed towards him, everything feminine in her drawn to his irresistible masculinity like an iron filing to a magnet. And then his arms were closing round her, enveloping her, crushing her unresisting softness against the rock face of his bone and sinew.

He groaned against her ear. 'Abby . . . oh Abby, I thought that scandal-sheet had spoilt everything for us. If I could've got hold of that reporter I'd have strangled him with my bare hands, dragging your name through his grubby columns. And instead I took out my frustration on you. . . .'

Her face was pressed into the curve of his neck and the scent, the taste of his skin was intoxicating. Blindly, mindlessly her fingers curled into his crisp hair while her mouth explored the curve of his jaw, his cheek, his chin. This couldn't be real. It had to be some fantasy conjured up by her longing. But when his mouth captured hers, almost brutal in its hunger, hurting, stopping her breath, it was so far outside her experience she knew she couldn't be imagining it. Instead of flinching from the pain he was inflicting her own hunger leapt to meet his, finding a wild satisfaction in abandoning herself to his crushing arms, his punishing domination.

He groaned deeply in his throat and as he did so his mouth gentled, no longer fiercely plundering but softening to a miraculous sweetness, moving over hers with a drugging sensuousness, clinging then moving again, parting her lips to taste the bruised softness of their inner sides. Without losing possession of her mouth his crushing embrace became a caress, his hands smoothing her back through the thin fabric of her robe, one sliding up over her shoulders to cup the nape of her neck, the other moving downwards, shaping her waist and on over the graceful curve of her hip, leaving a trail of tingling nerve ends, igniting a slow burning fire within her.

One hand still cupping the back of her head he drew back a little, looking down into her upturned face, his gaze travelling over her mouth, swollen from his kisses and tremulously inviting more, to her wide brown eyes still dazed from his assault on her senses and the depth of her own aroused emotions. His grey eyes had a curious brilliance and without releasing her from their gaze the arm that circled her hips tightened, drawing her forward, and at the same time he moved against her, blatantly showing her the strength of his arousal.

Abigail's eyes widened further in shock, but it was shock at herself as the slow burning fire inside her became a raging inferno at his touch and her own body moved against his in a yearning response. With a low growl of triumph Keir swept her suddenly boneless body into his arms and carried her to the bed, laying her down gently, her mane of fair hair spread like a cloud on the pillow. As he came down beside her his hands at once went to the belt of her robe but knowing she was naked underneath, instinctive shyness made her try to stop him.

He captured her hands, placing them on his shoulders and holding them there for several moments. 'No Abby, no false modesty. I want to look at you.'

Thick lashes swept down to veil her eyes though there was no hiding the blush staining her cheeks, but when his hands went back to deal quickly with the knot of her belt she let her own stay where he had put them. He pushed the concealing robe aside and feasted his eyes on the slender young body revealed. Against the black

of the outspread robe her pale skin had the translucence
of a pearl and her clamorous heartbeat was clearly
visible.

'God, Abby, but you're beautiful!' His voice was
husky, ragged, as if he was not quite in control of it and
beneath her hands she could actually feel him tremble.
Her heavy lashes lifted and she gazed at him in wonder
that innocent and inexperienced as she was, she could
actually shake that self-assured arrogance.

Then his hands began to move over her, stroking and
kneading possessively and she quivered like a perfectly
tuned violin string, mindless with delight, her breasts
seeming to leap and swell to fill his hands as he cupped
them.

'Touch me, Abby. Please touch me,' he begged, and
all shyness forgotten her fingers disposed of the buttons
of his shirt eagerly.

The skin of his shoulders and chest was as tanned as
his face and incredibly smooth, like supple satin
stretched over the rippling muscles, except where the
dark curling hair spread over his chest and veed to a
point at his navel. He gasped with pleasure at her touch
and again she was awed at her power to move him.

But it was when his mouth joined his hands in their
exploration of the most sensitive areas of her body that
her mind spiralled off into space leaving her at the
mercy of her physical responses. She arched towards
him, her short fingernails digging convulsively into his
muscled shoulders, her body no longer content to
submit to the delights of his lovemaking but answering
with a demanding passion of its own. Both his arms slid
beneath her as she arched, gathering her to him and the
roughness of his body hair against her hardened nipples
sent another almost unbearable wave of delight
coursing through her.

'I've imagined this ever since I set eyes on you,' Keir
murmured, mouth and tongue teasing her ear erotically
so that she writhed in desire, craving the fulfilment only

he could give. 'Breaking through that cool self-possession to the passionate woman underneath. But even I never dreamed it would be this good. I've never wanted any woman as much as I want you.'

He let her go abruptly and swinging his legs off the bed, began to unbuckle his belt. But it wasn't only the withdrawal of his body heat that made Abigail suddenly feel cold as he went on huskily, 'Hell, Abby, I've been *sick* with wanting you, especially these last four days! Why did you put us through that torment when you knew this was inevitable? Nearly two weeks wasted, and so little time left. . . .' He stood up to shrug off his pants.

He was magnificent. A wave of heat engulfed her, the heat of physical desire, but it couldn't warm the crust of ice his words had put around her heart. So little time left. . . . Keir wanted her but his wanting was an ephemeral thing. He could take her, satiate himself with her then happily wave her goodbye when she caught the plane back to London. If the last four days had been bleak and empty believing she would never see him again, what would her future be like, once she had known his full possession? She swept the edges of her robe together and rolled to the edge of the bed, swinging her legs to the floor.

Immediately the springs sagged as they took Keir's weight. 'Hey, you're not going cold on me now, Abby.' He was kneeling behind her, pulling her back against him so she could feel the heat of his nakedness through her thin robe, his hands fondling her shoulders, his voice lightly teasing, confident he could coax her out of her withdrawal.

Abigail shivered, fighting her treacherous body that still ached to surrender to him. 'I—I'm afraid——'

'Because you're still a virgin? Darling, don't you think I already realise that?' There was laughter in his voice but no mockery and when he twisted her round to face him there was such tenderness in his face that her defences rocked. He might look like that at the woman he loved. But if he *did* love her surely he'd be talking about the rest of their lives, not how short their time was?

'You mustn't be afraid,' he said softly. 'I'll be gentle, I promise. I won't hurt you. Abby, let me be the one to show you how wonderful loving can be. You do believe I can do that, don't you?'

'Yes, I know you can.' The words came out yearningly and Keir's possessive grip on her tightened.

'And you want me every bit as much as I want you? Your body's already told me as much so you might as well admit it.'

'Yes. . . .' It was a long sigh of admission.

'Well then?'

She almost succumbed, but when he went on to add huskily, 'I'll make it something you'll remember for the rest of your life, darling,' she twisted lithely away from him and he was so surprised he let her go.

'Perhaps that's what I'm afraid of.' Abigail fastened the robe securely then wrapped her arms tightly across her midriff as if to contain the pain that was tearing her apart, but it showed in her voice. 'I don't think I want to spend the rest of my life living on a memory.'

'I never took you for a tease, Abigail.' Keir's voice was muffled and when she glanced back at him he was lying on his stomach with his hands clasping his head as if he too was nursing a pain.

'You think that's what I've been doing? Teasing?' She was incredulous at the injustice of his accusation. 'You give me credit for more sophistication than I actually possess, Keir, and you under-rate your own attraction.' She turned away again to stare unseeingly out of the window.

The sound of him moving off the bed reached her but she didn't look round. Instead she burst out defensively, 'You should stick to your own league, Keir, ladies who know the score and who can take this kind of thing as lightly as you do, not waste your time with an old-fashioned girl like me who foolishly lets her feelings get involved.'

Keir said nothing but the soft sounds behind her still continued and she guessed he was dressing. A shaft of anguish made her tremble. He had been able to turn off so easily while her own body still ached for him, a physical pain.

Goaded beyond bearing she cried, 'What was I supposed to do, Keir, after you'd put your brand of possession on me then waved me goodbye? Be content with that one experience for the rest of my life, or seek out other men in the vain hope of finding one who could burn the memory of you away?'

The sounds behind her were suddenly stilled, and ashamed of that near hysterical outburst that had revealed far more than she'd intended she said wearily, 'I think you'd better go. I have a performance tonight and somehow I've got to try to get myself together again.'

She felt rather than heard his footfalls crossing the thick carpet and tensed, resisting as he gripped her shoulders and tried to turn her round. When he bent and lifted her, making a nonsense of her resistance, she gave a despairing cry and beat at him with her fists. But he only lowered her into an easy chair, kneeling in front of her, capturing her flying fists and imprisoning them in one hand while the other lifted her chin until she had to look into his clear grey eyes.

He said, 'Abigail, will you marry me?'

It was the crowning fantasy of a fantastic afternoon. If he had not been holding her chin so firmly her mouth would have dropped open with shock.

'Wh-what did you say?' she asked faintly, not daring to believe she had heard aright.

His mouth curved but his eyes devoured her. 'You heard, but as I've never said it before and never expect to say it again I don't mind repeating myself. Darling, I asked if you would marry me.'

A pulse beat frantically at the base of her throat and her dark eyes were hazed with bewilderment as she stared into his face. 'Marry you?' she whispered. Was he really offering what her heart and soul cried out for—a commitment? 'B . . . but I don't understand. A few minutes ago——'

'A few minutes ago I held you in my arms and I couldn't think of anything else but possessing you,' he broke in thickly.

'But——' The temptation to throw herself into his arms and tell him of course she would marry him was enormous, but somehow she managed to resist it. 'But you never made any secret of the fact that all you wanted was a brief affair.'

'Maybe I didn't look beyond an affair at first,' he admitted. 'I've never seen myself as a marrying man till now. But I don't know where you got hold of the idea it was to be brief.'

'You—you said yourself we had so little time.' He'd even used it as an argument to hasten her surrender.

He shook her gently. 'Until you fly back to London, you goose. Surely you knew I had every intention of following you? Didn't I tell you the night we first met I intended to spend a lot more time at Marmion in the future?'

Of course she remembered that conversation in the romantically gaslit restaurant when they'd discovered they had both of them connections with the little Leicestershire village of Great Wiston, but she didn't think he had.

He groaned. 'I suppose I can't blame you for looking so doubtful. I haven't exactly handled the situation with finesse, have I? But if all this is new ground to you, Abby, it's new to me too, believe me. Oh I'll admit I've wanted women before, but never the way I want you, and I've never felt so . . .' he fumbled for the right word,

'. . . so *possessive* as I feel with you. When that gossip columnist coupled your name with mine half of me was glad because it made us a pair, but the other half of me was disgusted with myself because I hadn't protected you better from snide innuendoes. I suppose it was then I knew deep down an affair with you wasn't going to be enough, but it really brought it home to me when you talked just now of using other men to make you forget me.'

His jaw hardened and a fierce look darkened his eyes. 'I've never believed myself possessive but, Hell! the very idea of another man as much as touching you. . . .'

The expression on his face, the emotion thickening his voice were utterly convincing and thrilled Abigail to the core. Surely it must mean that he loved her? Her mouth worked tremulously as she tried to contain her soaring, incredulous joy. 'You're really serious, Keir?' she whispered. 'You weren't just talking about marriage to make me feel better about sleeping with you?'

He actually winced, a dark red creeping over his cheekbones. 'You couldn't have thought——' He bit the words off. 'God, but I've given you a low opinion of me!'

He stood up, pulling her to her feet with him, gripping her shoulders lightly. 'Abby, if it'll convince you nothing like that ever crossed my mind, I promise I'll avoid situations like this, being alone together. I can't pretend it'll be easy but I won't try to make love to you again until we're married, if only you'll say yes.'

To hear him plead, to see his confidence so shaken touched her deeply. 'Oh Keir. . . .' There was tenderness in her fingers as she traced the strong lines of his face, a glowing happiness in her soft brown eyes and a shy surrender in the melting contours of her body as she went into his arms. 'Yes. Yes of course I'll marry you Keir, if you're quite sure that's what you want.'

He let out his breath as if he'd been holding it for a long time and Abigail felt the tremor that coursed through him. 'I've never been more sure of anything in my life, darling,' he assured her huskily. 'You and I belong together, Abby.'

He held her tightly but this time it was a protective rather than a hungry embrace, one hand pressing her cheek against his chest, his fingers laced through her silky hair, and when he finally released her it was with a light, fleeting kiss, as if he was holding himself in restraint.

'I know we ought to wait until we've told your grandmother,' he said, holding her away from him, 'but would you mind very much if we announced our engagement at the party after the concert tonight? I'd like to make sure this time that the gossip writers get the story right, and by the time the news filters through to England we should be back with your grandmother anyway.'

Abigail was incandescent that night, her happiness glowing in her dark eyes, shining from her radiant face, lighting a touch paper of excitement in her crowded audience before she even touched the keys of the piano. Never before had her playing shown quite such lyrical feeling, such depth of passion. The audience loved it, responding with a stunning crash of applause, recalling her to the platform time after time. But although her success thrilled and gratified her, it was as nothing compared to the thrill of pure joy at the proud, proprietorial look on Keir's face as he tucked her hand possessively under his arm and led her into the centre of the room at the reception afterwards.

All the guests had applauded her entrance but the sound died away to an interested buzz as Keir raised his hand. 'Ladies and gentlemen, we have an announcement to make. This lovely and talented lady only a few hours ago agreed to marry me, and just in case she should be having second thoughts by now, I'd like you all as witnesses——'

To Abigail's astonishment he pulled a small box from

his pocket and in full view of everyone, slid a magnificent sapphire surrounded by diamonds on to the third finger of her left hand. 'Keir . . .' she breathed. 'How on earth——?'

He smiled down at her, his eyes brilliant. 'The Minto name carries some clout. While you were dressing I contacted a friendly jeweller. You like it?'

She glanced down at the sparkling stones, the assurance of his love, and then looked back into his face, her heart in her eyes. 'It's quite, quite beautiful. Oh Keir . . . I love you so much.'

His eyes never leaving hers, he raised the palm of her hand to his lips. It was several moments before she became aware of the people pressing round them, offering their excited good wishes and congratulations.

'What about breaking the news to your family, Keir?' Abigail asked much later in the evening when they were sharing a quiet supper. 'Maybe I should give your parents the chance to look me over while I'm still in Canada. Your mother, I'm sure, will want to know the kind of girl she's getting for a daughter-in-law. If you like I could probably delay my flight home for a day or two.'

Something flickered in Keir's eyes. A certain wariness? But it was gone so quickly Abigail couldn't be sure she hadn't imagined it. 'There's no need to alter our plans, I've already called my folks with the news.' He took her hand, caressing the long fingers. 'It's more important to me to get your grandmother's blessing, Abby. I want to be sure there'll be no pressure from that quarter to make you change your mind.'

'Oh darling. . . .' Laughter bubbled up inside her like fizzy champagne. 'There's no chance of that, and why should Granny Lucy want to try? She'll love you as much as I do. Well, perhaps not *quite* as much.' Her dark eyes glowed, all the ardency of her newly discovered passionate nature revealed as she looked at him. 'When she knows how happy I am. . . .'

'If you love each other now, you won't love each other any less in three months' time.' Lucy Paston sat in her favourite high-backed wing chair, her faded blue eyes troubled.

On the sofa opposite, the increased pressure of Keir's grip on Abigail's hand betrayed his frustration.

They had flown back to London together and after a night's rest, Keir at his apartment and Abigail in her own small flat, he had collected her in his powerful black Porsche with the personalised number plate KM 100 and whisked her up the M1 to Great Wiston where Abigail had broken her exciting news. She had known it would come as a surprise but she had been confident that Granny Lucy would share in her happiness so the old lady's reservations had come as a shock and filled her with dismay.

'I've already waited thirty-five years for Abigail,' Keir said with such depth of feeling a delicious tingle rippled down Abigail's spine.

'Very romantic I'm sure,' her grandmother returned. 'But the fact remains you've only known each other for a couple of weeks.'

'Long enough to know I love him, Gran,' Abigail broke in quickly. 'To know he's the only man in the world for me.'

'I don't disbelieve you, child.' Granny Lucy's eyes flicked appreciatively to the forcefully attractive man at her granddaughter's side and she smiled. 'I'm not against this marriage, only against the unseemly haste. Indeed, I have no power to stop you marrying tomorrow if you've a mind. I suppose you *could* find time to fit in the ceremony between your engagements, Abigail?' she questioned dryly.

Abigail flushed. 'We hadn't actually got down to choosing a date.'

'In other words, you've neither of you come down out of the clouds long enough to consider any of the practicalities.' Granny Lucy leaned forward and fixed her prospective grandson-in-law with an unwavering gaze. 'For instance you, Keir, apparently have business commitments that necessitate a certain amount of travelling—and so does Abigail. Or are you expecting her to give up her career when she marries you?'

'No, of course not,' he denied at once. 'Though I would hope——' his eyes travelled possessively over the girl at his side, '—that you'll be able to arrange things so we don't have to be apart *too* often, Abby.' Then as if feeling the old lady's sharply sardonic gaze on him he added stiffly, 'Though I can see there'll have to be compromises on both sides.'

'And what about you, Abby?' Granny Lucy pressed. 'Will you really be happy to leave a brand new husband and go flying of to—where is it next? Germany?'

Abigail's agonised gaze flew to Keir's face. She knew very well she wouldn't.

The old lady hauled herself to her feet and crossed the rug to stand before them, taking their joined hands in her own arthritic ones. 'Am I really asking too much, suggesting you wait for three months?' she said quietly.

Keir's mouth curved into a reluctant grin. 'I guess not, Granny Lucy, but don't blame me too much for being impatient to tie your lovely granddaughter down.' He pulled Abigail to her feet, an arm circling each of them as if taking them into his protection. His grin widened. 'Now I know where Abby inherited her persuasive tongue,' he teased.

'And *I* know how Abby came to find herself swept off her feet,' the old lady sparkled back at him.

Abigail's eyes widened. She'd never seen her grandmother actually flirtatious before. Then she too smiled. The two people she loved best in the world had accepted each other, had already begun to like each other. And three months wasn't so very long to wait until she could belong to Keir.

They stayed to lunch at Mill House and then leaving

Granny Lucy to her afternoon nap, Keir drove Abigail the short distance to Marmion. Her anticipation at finally seeing inside the house she had always liked so much was slightly tempered as they drew up beside a white two-seater sports car parked in the drive.

'It looks as if you have a visitor,' she said, but Keir only laughed.

'Oh the car? It belongs to my secretary. I phoned her last night and asked her to be here. I want her to meet you and——' he grimaced '——I'm afraid there's going to be work for me to catch up on.'

Abigail's eyes widened as Keir handed her out of the Porsche and she was able to get a closer look at the sports car. She couldn't help commenting, 'You must be a very generous employer if your secretary can afford to drive this.'

Keir grinned. 'I am, but she's worth every penny. A very efficient lady indeed.' He took her arm and led her inside. 'Come on, darling. Come and inspect your future home.'

Abigail forgot everything as she gazed around the wide hall, the sun pouring in through the big window at the top of the graceful staircase and gleaming on the polished oak floor. For a house Keir admitted he had spent little time in as yet, it had a very lived-in atmosphere. The reason for that became apparent when a door to the left of the hall opened to reveal a well-equipped kitchen and a stout, motherly lady bustled out.

'My housekeeper, Mrs Jameson, Abby,' Keir said, slipping a possessive arm around Abigail's shoulders. 'Jamie, let me introduce you to the future Mrs Minto.'

Abigail was warmed by the housekeeper's delighted welcome and thought she detected a certain satisfaction in that lady's voice when, after offering her congratulations and good wishes she said, 'Does Miss Wilde know about this good news yet?'

'Does Miss Wilde know about *what* good news?' a cool voice inquired.

Abigail turned and framed in an arched doorway leading off from the back of the hall stood the most beautiful woman she had ever seen; long glossy dark red hair, exotically slanting, almond-shaped green eyes and a full, sensuous mouth in a heart-shaped face, a sinuous, seductive grace in the small-boned, dainty figure.

'Ah, there you are.' Smiling, Keir drew Abigail towards this vision of loveliness. 'This is the very efficient lady I was telling you about, Abby, my secretary, Zena Wilde. Zena, I'd like you to meet Abigail Paston.' His possessive arm tightened still more around her shoulders. 'Abby and I are engaged to be married, Zena.'

'Married!' The shock in the other girl's slanting green eyes was unmistakable and so was the sudden, wincing pain.

Abigail's own eyes widened in understanding. Loving Keir as she did and acutely aware of his devastating, magnetic attraction, she could feel for this girl's pain. She glanced up at Keir. Did he know his secretary was in love with him?

His next words seemed to indicate that he was quite unaware of it. 'I want to show Abby around the house so she can decide on any changes she wants to make.' He drew her past the still stunned secretary and into the big, sun-filled sitting room. 'I know three months seems an eternity to wait——' the grey eyes looking down into her upturned face were intimately hungry, and then he smiled with a touch of wry humour, '—but if the mayhem of preparations for my sister's wedding was anything to go by, there'll be a million and one things to be done. Maybe you'll be able to help us out with the arrangements, Zena,' he tossed over his shoulder, 'especially as Abby has a full book of professional engagements.'

If he noticed his secretary's silence he ignored it. 'Now, what do you think of this room, darling?'

Sofa and chairs upholstered in old gold velvet stood grouped before a stone fireplace, blending in perfectly with the Oriental carpet patterned in golds and blues on a white background. Matching comfortable chairs stood round a circular low table on the raised dais of a huge curved window taking up most of the longest wall in the room while at one end French windows hung with the same rich damask curtains to match the upholstery led out on to a sheltered terrace and from there to lawns sweeping down to the stream. At the opposite end of the room a door stood open to reveal a study—obviously where Zena had been working when they arrived—and the rest of that wall was taken up by well-filled bookshelves and Keir's stereo equipment and record collection.

'Keir, it's beautiful!' Abigail stood looking round her with delight. 'I've always liked this house but it's even lovelier inside than I imagined. I can't think of a thing I'd want to alter in here.'

Keir looked pleased. 'Not even the addition of a piano?' he suggested teasingly. 'I thought if we moved those things out of the bay, that would be the ideal spot for it, up on the dais.'

'Darling, it sounds splendid, but don't you think my poor old baby grand might look like a poor relation in here? It's rather battered.' She laughed up at him. 'Besides, the sound of me practising could drive you mad when you're trying to work in your study.'

'Then I'll have to buy you a new one, won't I?' he said blandly.

'Keir! I wasn't——' Abigail broke off in stunned confusion. Did he have any idea how much a new grand piano would cost? She didn't think he could have and she didn't want him to think she'd been angling for him to buy her one.

'Whoever heard of a pianist without a piano, and as I hope we'll spend a lot of our time here, of course you must have one.' He took her hands, drawing her against him. 'Let me do this for you, Abby. Let's call it my wedding present to you. And as for your practising getting on my nerves—I'll never get tired of hearing you play.'

Abigail melted at the tenderness of his expression. Incredible that such a strong, dominant face could look so tender or that grey eyes could hold so much warmth! She forgot everything but her overwhelming love for him.

It was Zena's brittle voice that brought her down to earth. 'Forgive me for introducing a note of realism but you're going to lose that Bonnington contract if you don't do something about it today, Keir. I've been holding them off but knowing you were back I promised Mr Halstead you'd ring him this afternoon and you still have the final figures to go through yet.'

Keir sighed regretfully. 'She's right I'm afraid, darling. Look, I'll get Mrs Jameson to show you the rest of the house and give you some tea. How's that?'

Abigail smilingly agreed but she was aware of the angry satisfaction in Zena's green eyes as the secretary closed the study door behind herself and Keir, and a cold finger touched Abigail's spine.

CHAPTER FIVE

THE housekeeper was only too glad to take Abigail under her motherly wing and proudly showed off her gleaming kitchen before taking her on a tour of the rest of the house; the dining room with its turkey red carpet and the gleam of silver and crystal against the dark, polished table, the sweeping staircase with its spacious, sunny landing, two pretty, chintzy guest rooms and the bathroom tiled in old rose.

'This is the room Miss Wilde uses when she's here,' Mrs Jameson said as she pushed open a third door, adding with a note of disapproval, 'Not the tidiest of young ladies, and she only arrived this morning.'

Abigail noted it was larger than the two bedrooms she had already seen and it was certainly disordered. Cosmetics and perfume littered the dressing table in untidy profusion. A sheer black nightdress had been thrown on to the lilac bedcover while a matching négligé had half slithered off the dressing-table stool where it had been tossed. A suede coat and a handbag had been dumped on a chair and discarded tights lay on the deeper lilac carpet beside a pair of shoes that had just been stepped out of and left. A crumpled newspaper and a hair dryer lay on another chair while the distinctive perfume Zena used still hung in the air.

The room gave Abigail an uneasy feeling, as if the other girl, by deliberately strewing her belongings around, was stamping it with her possession.

'You don't live in then, Mrs Jameson?' she asked, relieved to move out and close the door.

'Not actually in, no. Me and Dick—that's my husband who looks after the garden—we have the flat over the garages. Nice and handy but a place of our own, like.' Mrs Jameson opened the last door and stood aside. 'Now this is the master bedroom where Mr Keir sleeps.'

After the feminine clutter of Zena's room, this one looked almost austere. The two large windows which pierced one wall, hung with pine-green curtains, and the ivory carpet and plain ivory walls where a few very good pictures were displayed to advantage accentuated the sense of spaciousness and light.

'This bedroom has its own bathroom through here.' Mrs Jameson pushed open the door and Abigail saw the same ivory and pine-green colour scheme was carried through in its luxurious fixtures and fittings.

She turned back to the bedroom. The furniture was in a light polished wood, the wardrobes built in along one entire wall. Two silver-backed man's hairbrushes lay on the dressing table and a group of photographs in leather frames stood on top of the chest of drawers, photographs Abigail would have liked to study as she guessed they were of his family. The bedhead in matching light wood was fitted with a stereo tape deck and bookshelves but it was the bed itself that drew Abigail's eyes. A big, king-size bed, its duvet covered in the same pine green to match the curtains.

The bed she would one day share with Keir.

Abigail felt a warmth stirring inside her, curling through her with licking fingers as she remembered his lovemaking and the bed they had almost shared in Toronto.

Keir had promised then he would stop trying to persuade her to let him make love to her until they were safely married. Would he keep that promise she wondered? Did she really *want* him to keep it?

Two days later Keir was driving her back to London. She had not seen a great deal of him; as he had warned, he had a lot of work to catch up on and had spent many hours shut in his study with his lovely secretary. But Abigail had not minded too much. Her grandmother was delighted to have her company and wanted to hear all about the tour and how Abigail had come to meet and fall in love with Keir. And anyway, Keir had found time to take her to a surprisingly good restaurant on the fringe of the village that specialised in French cooking, and together they had visited the vicar to make arrangements for their marriage in Great Wiston parish church at the end of September.

'I feel we're getting somewhere now we've got the wedding date fixed,' Keir said with obvious satisfaction as they sped along the M1. 'So what about deciding where you want to go for your honeymoon?'

Her honeymoon! The time when she and Keir would be entirely alone with all restraints removed. The now familiar melting warmth that was half pleasurable, half an unbearable ache, curled through her.

'Perhaps we should send Mr and Mrs Jameson away and shut ourselves in at Marmion?' she suggested, only half-joking.

His eyes caressed her briefly before going back to the road. 'You like the house, then?'

'Oh yes.' She snuggled down even further into her seat. 'How could anyone *not* love it?'

'I'm glad. Unfortunately as well as getting rid of the Jamesons we'd also have to have the phone and the doorbell disconnected,' he said wryly. 'Too many of my business colleagues would know where to find me.'

'Then as I have no intention of sharing my honeymoon with your business, maybe we *should* think again,' she returned promptly.

He grinned. 'And as I have no intention of sharing you either, how does Bermuda grab you? A friend of mine has a villa there we could have. *Very* secluded.'

A wave of breathless happiness gave her the sensation of floating. How had she got so lucky? To have a man like Keir wanting to share the rest of his life with her, a man who with that charismatic attraction could have taken his pick of the society butterflies of two continents, not to mention his own very lovely secretary! Sometimes she couldn't quite believe it was all happening.

'It sounds heavenly.' The breadth and depth of her love for him put an emotional huskiness into her voice. 'Though quite frankly, I don't care where we go. As long as we're together it could be on a rocket to the moon.'

'You choose the damndest time to say a thing like that.' His voice was taut and his hands whitened on the steering wheel as he overtook a thundering truck.

Abigail's eyes flew to his face, wide and disconcerted. 'Why?'

'Why? My darling girl, speeding down the motorway is *not* the best time to be overcome by a powerful urge to make love to you.'

'Oh Keir. . . .' She smiled up at him mistily, her feelings too deep to be expressed in words.

That soaring, blazing happiness carried her along on golden wings for the next four weeks. Not that she saw as much of Keir as she would have liked, but she had a full programme of concert and recital engagements and Keir too had to spend some time away, visiting his electronics factories in the North and in the West Midlands. But he managed to be there for all her London concerts and to just a few in the provinces, and beside supporting her at as many professional engagements as he could, he squired her with possessive pride to the parties and charity functions that were part of her musical world and introduced her to a world that was new to her, that of his own, introducing her to many of his business friends and colleagues.

In spite of being so busy she still found time to make several flying visits to see her grandmother and to get some of the preparations under way for the wedding they had decided to keep as small and intimate as possible; booking a room in a hotel not far from Great Wiston for the small reception, ordering the invitations and the wedding cake. She also made time to visit Serge to share some of her delirious happiness with her old teacher and to ask him, as the nearest person to a male relative of her own, to give her away at her wedding, a task the old man was delighted and honoured to take on, only regretting that Abigail hadn't been able to bring her husband-to-be with her so he could see for himself whether this young man was worthy of his favourite.

If there was a tiny cloud on her happiness it was Zena's proprietorial attitude towards Keir, the other girl's superior knowledge of Keir's world and the ease with which she made Abigail feel out of her depth and inadequate in it. But Abigail tried to be charitable, knowing how hurt Zena must feel, how hard it must be for her to accept that the man she loved was marrying someone else.

It wasn't always easy to be charitable. In fact the way Zena took the shine out of Keir's wonderful wedding gift to her made it very hard indeed.

Abigail had given a Friday lunchtime recital in the Leicester Museum Art Gallery and was naturally staying overnight with her grandmother. It was towards the evening of that day when Keir, who she had believed to be in London, turned up at Mill House in a mood of suppressed excitement and insisted on driving her over to Marmion.

As soon as she walked into the sitting room there she realised the cause of his secretively excited mood. Standing on the dais in the big bow window was a magnificent white Bechstein piano!

'Oh Keir. . . .' Breathlessly she slid on to the stool and ran her fingers over the keys, listening to the perfect tone, then springing up again she flung her arms around him, her eyes glowing, her face alive with delight. 'Thank you darling. It's the most fabulous wedding present any girl could wish for.'

His strong mouth curved with a tenderness that

melted her bones and the tiny lines at the corners of his eyes deepened in amusement at her heady delight. 'Better than diamonds?' he teased.

'Oh a million times better.' She drew his head down and kissed the little scar above his lip, and instantly his arms tightened round her, his mouth capturing hers in a deep, hungrily searching kiss. They were both shaken, both breathing raggedly by the time he reluctantly released her.

'I think I'd better book a table for us at La Maison tonight,' he said thickly. 'If we eat here there's no way I'm going to be able to stop myself anticipating our wedding night.'

Still dazed with the passion he had aroused in her, Abigail gazed back at him, her heart swelling inside her with love until it was almost a physical pain, her senses clamouring to know this man completely, to commit herself to him wholly, to find the fulfilment she knew only he could give her.

Her lips parted to tell him, but she hesitated too long. He kissed the tip of her nose and held her at arms' length. 'You try out your piano while I go and change. I shan't be long.' He turned and walked swiftly from the room.

Abigail returned to the piano stool and took a deep breath, trying to compose her tumultuous emotions, but before she could touch the keys an uncomfortable prickling at the back of her neck had her twisting round to see Zena watching her from the doorway of the study. Self-conscious colour rose in her cheeks. How long had Keir's secretary been standing there? How much of that strictly private scene had she overheard? Most of it, Abigail guessed, from the hard, angry glitter of the other girl's eyes.

'Don't you think it could be bad luck, accepting your wedding present so long before the event?' Zena said with malicious spite. 'Especially as this marriage is doomed from the start.'

Abigail's eyes widened in shock. 'I don't know why you should say that!'

'Oh come on. . . .' Zena's laugh was as brittle as glass. 'It's like mating a mouse with a tom cat! You're a novelty to Keir at the moment but you're worlds apart. What do you really have in common? I know and understand Keir better than you ever will.'

The shaking started inside and it took all Abigail's control to say evenly, 'You've known Keir a long time, I suppose.'

The pointed chin came up arrogantly and the green eyes flashed. 'Three years. Don't flatter yourself *you'll* last that long.'

Abigail's hands were clasped so tightly in her lap that the knuckles gleamed white and her sapphire and diamond engagement ring bit into her flesh. 'Three years? And don't you think that in all that time Keir had ample opportunity to deepen your relationship from secretary and employer—if he'd wanted to?'

The other girl's sinuous figure stiffened in anger. 'You know *nothing* about our relationship, nothing! Let me tell you I know him far more intimately than he's ever admitted to *you*.' The study door reverberated as Zena turned on her heel and slammed it shut behind her.

Abigail let out a long, shaky breath, feeling rather limp and sick. Was it true what Zena had implied, that she and Keir had been lovers? From his determined pursuit of herself across Canada and some of the remarks he had made while trying to seduce her into his bed she couldn't pretend to herself that he would have held back from any moral scruples. That his past relationships with women had been 'adult' he had never tried to conceal. When he was attracted to a woman he didn't hesitate to follow that attraction through to its logical conclusion. And his secretary was a very beautiful woman.

It was devastating, the anguish that coursed through

her at the thought of Zena in Keir's arms, sharing his bed, enjoying his lovemaking. It took quite a time to get a grip on herself, to remind herself that it was no good worrying over Keir's past. It was *now* that mattered, and the future—*their* future, hers and Keir's. So she must let common sense prevail and see that nasty scene for what it was, the jealous outburst of a girl who was having to witness the man she loved marrying someone else. But even then she couldn't quite recapture her pleasure in Keir's wedding gift or her former delirious happiness.

The fact that Keir was sending Zena back to London that night while remaining for the weekend at Marmion himself did something to take away the nasty taste Zena's spiteful allegations had left in Abigail's mouth and when on Sunday morning he accompanied Granny Lucy and herself to church to hear the banns for their marriage read for the first time, she couldn't help reaching impulsively for his hand. Of *course* he wasn't marrying her because she was a novelty. And they *did* have a lot in common, not least their mutual love of music. And anyway, how many wives had any real idea of the cut-and-thrust business world their husbands moved in?

And as for Zena's other distasteful hint—she tensed her muscles and willed it not to hurt—maybe Keir *had* made love to his secretary sometime during their three-year association, but not any more, not now.

On Monday morning Keir returned to London while Abigail stayed on at Great Wiston as the following day she had to be at the television studios in Birmingham to be interviewed for a news magazine programme, so it was Wednesday before she saw him again. He took her out for a quiet dinner before returning her to her flat.

'Can't have you flaking out on the platform of the Albert Hall, so I'm making sure you get an early night.' He was referring to her engagement the following night as soloist at one of the Henry Wood Promenade Concerts.

Abigail smiled up at him tremulously. The pace was getting her down a bit and she was not seeing as much of Keir as she wished she could.

So she wasn't pleased when he came to her dressing room after the performance to see his secretary hanging on to his arm.

'I've been widening Zena's education,' he grinned, disengaging Zena's clutching fingers to kiss Abigail lightly. 'She happened to mention she'd never heard you play.'

Abigail hid her tension behind a mask of politeness. 'Oh? I hope you weren't disappointed, Zena.'

The other girl shrugged. 'You didn't play any wrong notes—as far as I could judge.'

'You see, a complete Philistine.' Keir's grin widened.

'Not at all.' Zena's eyebrows rose coolly. 'It's just that my tastes lean more to the visual—ballet, opera, theatre.'

Her sharp eyes saw Keir's attention being claimed by Lady Elizabeth Dornfield, one of the many well-wishers beginning to arrive in Abigail's dressing room to offer their congratulations, and she added with a complacent smile, 'When Keir takes me out it's usually to something more adult and sophisticated than a promenade concert—all those dedicated beardless boys pressing to the front! Like the nightclub we went to on Tuesday.'

While Abigail herself had been out of the way in Birmingham? The jealous thought stabbed. Keir hadn't mentioned going to any nightclub when he'd seen her last night.

She was aware of Zena watching closely for the effect of her words and tried desperately hard not to let her uncertainty show, risking instead taking a calculated gamble. 'Oh, that would be when he needed your help to entertain those businessmen, I suppose,' she said,

YOURS FREE

4 Harlequin Romances® and a fashion tote

It's our way of introducing you to our Harlequin Reader Service that's so much easier and less expensive than buying your novels retail.

As a subscriber, you'll receive 6 new books to preview every month. Always before they're available in stores. Always for the same low price. Always with the right to return the shipment and owe nothing.

R7MU

▸▸▸ FREE BOOKS & TOTE BAG ◂◂◂

YES, please send me 4 **FREE** Harlequin Romances and my **FREE** tote bag. Then send me 6 new Harlequin Romances each month. Bill me for only $1.65 each (for a total of $9.95 per shipment—a saving of $1.75 off retail price). There are no shipping, handling or other hidden charges. I can cancel anytime. The 4 free novels and tote bag are mine to keep, even if I never buy a book from Harlequin.

116 CIR EAXG

NAME_____

ADDRESS_____ APT._____

CITY_____

STATE_____ ZIP_____

Offer limited to one per household and not valid for present subscribers. Prices subject to change.

As a Harlequin Subscriber, you'll receive free . . .

- our monthly newsletter
  HEART TO HEART
- our magazine
  ROMANCE DIGEST
- bonus books and gifts
- special edition Harlequin Best Sellers to
  preview for 10 days without obligation

DETACH AND MAIL TODAY

RUSH

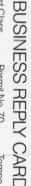

and congratulated herself on putting just the right casual interest into her voice.

The hard flash in Zena's eyes brought a sense of relief as she guessed she had hit on the truth, but then the other girl's mouth curved into a secretive smile. 'Oh, is *that* what he told you?'

Abigail gnawed her lip as the other girl turned away. Should she ask Keir about it, or should she dismiss it as just so much jealous troublemaking? The last thing she wanted was to give Keir the impression she didn't trust him. She worried about it all over supper, showing so little of her usual appetite that Keir was quite concerned.

'It's just that it's an ordeal, playing in the Albert Hall, especially knowing the radio microphones and television cameras are on you too,' she excused herself as he handed her into the black Porsche.

They were drawing up in front of her block of flats before she broached the subject that had really taken her appetite, and although she tried to keep her voice light, to treat it as if it was of little consequence when she said, 'I hear you've been nightclubbing while I was away,' her tension must have been evident because Keir looked at her sharply.

'So that's why you've been sulking! Yes, a business contact turned up in London who had to be entertained. You would've been included too if you'd been around, so there's no need to behave as if I've committed some heinous offence.'

Abigail flinched, the tone of his voice lashing her like the flick of a whip. 'I . . . I'm sorry. Of course you've committed no offence. It's just that—well, hearing it from Zena like that made it sound——'

'I'm sure she'd never have mentioned it if she'd had the slightest idea it would provoke this display of jealousy,' he broke in coldly, and Abigail stared at him in dismay.

She *had* been jealous, it was no good denying it, and

it had been exactly what Zena intended. But now Keir was acting as if it was Abigail herself who had committed some crime!

Deeply troubled she said reluctantly, 'Keir . . . you do realise Zena's in love with you?'

She hadn't really known what reaction to expect from him but it certainly wasn't the contemptuous distaste the street light revealed in his face or the clipped anger when he said, 'My secretary's feelings—or lack of them—have nothing to do with us, Abigail. I can only put this outburst down to the fact that you're overtired and overwrought, but I hope you're not going to make a habit of allowing your imagination such a free rein.'

He got out of the car before she could defend herself and she numbly allowed him to escort her to the door of her flat where he pulled her into his arms and kissed her hard, a kiss without tenderness, intended to punish.

'Goodnight, Abigail. I'll see you tomorrow.' His face still hard and angry he turned and walked away.

Feeling bereft and oddly frightened, Abigail got ready for bed, but drained and exhausted as she was, sleep wouldn't come. Why had Keir been so angry? Surely she had had justification for being upset and jealous the way Zena had told her of the outing to the nightclub, and if it had been as innocent as Keir maintained, then why hadn't he told her about it himself?

Perhaps she should have tried to explain more lucidly her suspicions that Zena was attempting to cause trouble between them, but then Keir's coldly contemptuous distaste when she had asked him if he was aware of his secretary's feelings for him had frozen any explanation before it could be uttered. The memory of his contempt still chilled her and she couldn't help wishing fervently that she *hadn't* risen to Zena's bait and brought up the question of the nightclub.

Facing Keir's anger had been a devastating experience, filling her with a shivering, sick apprehension, making her feel lost and vulnerable, as abandoned as if he had withdrawn his love from her. And it was even more frightening not understanding *why* he'd been so angry.

She slept badly, her dreams full of dark forebodings, and woke later than usual in the morning heavy-headed, with shadows beneath her eyes. Pulling on a thin cotton robe she padded on bare feet into the tiny, primrose painted kitchen, hoping a cup of hot black coffee would make her feel more alive. While waiting for the percolator she took down a packet of cereal and a bowl from the cupboard and then replaced them again, admitting the impossibility of trying to eat while the sick feeling of apprehension still had her in knots.

Taking her coffee through to the sitting room she picked up the score of a new work she was adding to her repertoire, but a re-run of that disturbing scene with Keir kept coming between her and her study of the music. She felt tempted to phone Keir to apologise. Anything to set things right between them again. But apologise for what? She still had no clear idea of what had made Keir lose his temper, so how could she set things right? And anyway the thought of having to go through Zena to speak to him, perhaps having his secretary overhear at least Keir's end of the conversation, made her shrink.

It was a day without any professional engagements and it stretched long and empty in front of her with only her troubled thoughts for company. The flat was suddenly stifling. Out of consideration to the other tenants she restricted her practising here to an hour in the morning and another in the afternoon, but today that wasn't going to be enough.

Just for a moment she thought longingly of the beautiful new piano at Marmion and how there would be no restrictions on her hours of practice there, but that brought back the memory of Zena's upsetting remarks. What she needed was some really concentrated work to occupy her *now*.

She showered quickly and dressed in a crisp honey-coloured cotton dress, tying her heavy fair hair back in the nape of her neck with a matching scarf, then picking up the new score and her purse she left the flat. It wasn't until she had turned into the side street nearby where she usually parked her Mini car that she remembered she had left it at the garage in Great Wiston for a long-overdue service as she wouldn't be needing it while she was away on her German tour. Irritated, she had to search out a cab to take her to Chelsea where she knew she could practice as long and hard as she liked on one of her old teacher's pianos.

The therapy worked. It was a difficult modern piece of music and she immersed herself in it with all her concentrated determination. If Serge glanced at her searchingly whenever he looked in and wondered what it was that was driving her so hard, he made no comment, other than to ask again as she left when she would bring her fiancé to meet him.

Dressing that evening for a party at Lady Dornfield's house and waiting for Keir to collect her, her nerves returned in full force. Although she had spent time and care over her appearance—styling her hair in a sophisticated knot on the crown of her head and choosing a clinging black gown with a low-cut bodice and diaphanous sleeves to set off the contrast of dark eyes and tawny fair hair—she paused nervously in front of the mirror before going to the door to let him in, for the first time her joyful anticipation at seeing him mixed with a sinking apprehension. Would he still be angry with her?

Her heart was beating fast, her smile uncertain, her eyes huge with trepidation as she looked up at him.

He was smiling, his grey eyes warmly appreciative as they slid slowly over her. 'Mmm, you look good enough to eat.'

Her heart jolted and seemed to turn over inside her as he pulled her gently into his arms and kissed her with all the tenderness that had been missing last night. Weak with relief that he had forgotten his anger she melted against him, responding with an ardour that surprised them both.

'Hey, that was some welcome!' he teased, his hand cupping her face, his thumb brushing her mouth. 'I reckon you'll have to freshen up your lipstick when you fetch your wrap.' But when she went to move away to do as he suggested he pulled her back. 'But not just yet. There's a little bit of pink there I haven't eaten off yet.' His mouth swooped down again to recapture hers, teasing, tasting, dominating, reducing her bones to pliant rubber, making her cling to him in a dizzying haze of happiness.

In the car driving to Dornfield House she half expected him to make some comment on the way they had parted last night, even perhaps to apologise for his unkindness. But he said nothing, and neither did he mention the subject the whole evening, though he was so possessively attentive to her she wondered if that was by way of making up for the harsh words he had spoken. For herself, Abigail was far too happy to risk saying anything to remind him of their brief discord.

The following week Abigail had to leave for her concert tour of Germany. Keir saw her off at the airport, regretful that he was too busy himself to get away to accompany her.

'Take care of yourself, honey, and don't work yourself into the ground,' he said huskily, holding her close as her flight was called.

'You too,' Abigail whispered, and her eyes swam with tears. 'Oh Keir . . . I'm going to miss you so. . . .' It was like dying a little, parting from him.

'You'll call me often?' he said urgently, and she nodded.

'Every night, I promise.'

Her first concert was a tremendous success, the Frankfurt audience taking the fragilely fair girl with the enormous talent to their hearts. They were touchingly eager to show their appreciation and Abigail had to school herself not to show her impatience to get away to the privacy of her hotel room so she could phone Keir and share her triumph with him.

Only when she finally managed to put her call through to his London apartment it was not Keir who answered, but Zena.

'Abigail!' The secretary's usually confident tones sounded oddly disconcerted. 'Oh dear!' She gave what could only be described as a nervous giggle. 'I don't think Keir was expecting you to call this late. He's taking a shower. Hang on, I'll see if he can come to the phone.'

Abigail glanced at her watch. It *was* late as she had had difficulty in getting away from her hospitable German hosts, but if nearly midnight was late for her to be calling Keir, wasn't it also late for Zena to still be at Keir's apartment?

'Darling! How did it go?' Keir's warm voice crackled eagerly over the line.

'What's Zena doing at your apartment at this time of night?' She hadn't meant to say that. Certainly she hadn't meant to sound so accusing.

The silence bristled, and then, 'What do you think she's doing?' he said, his voice dangerously quiet. 'Working, of course.'

'Working!' She hadn't meant to sound so sceptical either but hadn't been able to help herself.

'It's what I pay her for.' There was no trace of the eager lover now in the hard, flat voice. 'Now are you going to tell me how the concert went or do you mean to continue this stupid inquisition?'

'I ... I'm sorry. I was just surprised when she answered. . . .' With great difficulty Abigail tore her mind away from the note almost of guilt in Zena's voice that still seemed to be ringing in her ears and went on to tell him of her success, but somehow the triumph she had so looked forward to sharing with him was suddenly hollow.

As she lay in bed that night in the impersonal hotel room she tried to tell herself Keir had every right to be annoyed at her suspicions. He payed Zena a very high salary so naturally he expected more of her than he would from a nine-to-five secretary.

Like finding comfort and amusement in her arms? a little demon voice whispered in her ear.

No! Keir wouldn't do that. He might have done so once but not now, not when he loved her, Abigail. And he *did* love her, didn't he, even if he'd never actually said it? After all they were getting married in another six weeks. She was being unjust to him, she told herself severely, reading too much into Zena's manner, the tone of her voice.

But there were too many times during that tour when she phoned Keir late at night only to have the calls answered by Zena, her voice husky and somehow *sated*, to prevent the ugly, agonising doubts returning. She didn't *want* to give them credence. Dear God, she loved Keir so much. Even thinking about him made her ache for him body and soul.

His greeting, his hungry kiss when he met her off the plane on her return to London dispelled her doubts for a time, but Zena's smug complacency when the two girls met seemed to negate the loving reassurance of his arms.

Abigail was ashamed of her suspicions, too ashamed of them to voice them. Keir would have every reason to be furious with her if they weren't true, to be disappointed in her lack of trust. But if they were true? She grew tense and jumpy, managing to keep her jealous questions bottled up but unable to hide her dislike of the other girl, often bringing a frown to Keir's dark brows by her stiff antagonism.

'For heaven's sake, Abby, why have you got it in for Zena?' he demanded one day when she had abruptly turned down his suggestion that she should let his secretary take some of the weight of the wedding arrangements off her shoulders.

'Because I'm afraid she means more to you than a mere secretary should,' she wanted to shout at him, but fear of having her doubts about their relationship confirmed kept her silent.

And then in one traumatic weekend they were doubts no longer. It began badly. After a long, tiring day spent recording some Beethoven sonatas, Keir phoned her at the studios where he was supposed to be collecting her to say he was going to be delayed and suggesting she took a cab to his office when she was through.

'The great man's still in conference,' Zena said when Abigail finally walked into the tastefully furnished outer office of the executive suite at the top of the Minto Enterprises London building, nodding towards an inner door from behind which came the subdued murmur of voices. 'You'd better sit down, you look fagged out.' The green eyes studied her, maliciously critical. 'But then we both know what a virilely demanding lover Keir is, don't we?'

Abigail gasped in shock. Zena was *admitting* she and Keir were lovers? Her legs suddenly unable to support her, she sank into the chair the secretary had indicated.

Zena's eyes narrowed as she watched Abigail's shocked, flaming face. 'Does this maidenly display of embarrassment mean you're *not* lovers? Well——' she leaned back in her chair. 'That explains a lot. You're a lot brighter than I gave you credit for, Abigail, holding out for marriage. But not as clever as you *think* you are.' Her voice hardened to a jeering note. 'Keir's an experienced man, my dear, and he's always had a taste for variety, so don't run away with the idea that your innocent, ingenuous charms are going to hold him in thrall for long.'

Abigail licked her dry lips, 'I don't believe you,' she croaked.

'You don't believe what?' Zena's fine eyebrows rose and her cat's eyes gleamed. 'That Keir's a fantastic lover or that you can't hold him?'

'You shouldn't be talking to me like this.' Abigail sprang to her feet. 'I won't listen to you——'

Just then the inner door opened. As if aware of the electric tension in the atmosphere Keir darted a narrowed glance at the two women but made no comment until he had escorted his visitor out, then turning back to them he rapped, 'Have you two been quarrelling?'

Before Abigail could open her mouth Zena was saying smoothly, 'I'm afraid your fiancée was a little— upset. But I *do* understand, Keir. Abigail's had a bad day and as a prospective bride she's under some considerable strain anyway, so I'm not about to take offence.'

Keir's hard, contemptuous glance pierced Abigail to the heart and she could only stare back at him helplessly. How could she defend herself when Zena had cut the ground so neatly from beneath her feet? If she told Keir exactly what Zena had claimed—that he and she were lovers—she had no doubt the other girl would be able to twist that too to her own advantage, or even deny she'd said any such thing. And the way Keir was looking at her now, there didn't seem much doubt whose version of the argument he would believe!

It didn't help to learn that Zena was travelling down to Great Wiston with them, or that Zena—under the pretext that Abigail would be able to rest more easily in the back of the car—took possession of the front passenger seat without any objection from Keir.

It was a miserable journey for Abigail, half listening to the murmur of voices from the front discussing business interminably, with only the odd remark tossed in her direction now and again over Keir's shoulder.

There was no opportunity either for her to set the record straight when they arrived, as instead of dropping Zena at Marmion first and so giving Abigail a short time alone with him, Keir drove straight to Mill House.

It was dark when they turned into the sloping drive and a new uneasiness feathered down Abigail's spine, pushing her lacerated feelings into the background.

'There are no lights on, Keir,' she said as she got out of the car.

'Your grandmother *was* expecting you, I suppose?' He too looked frowningly towards the dark house as he went to the boot to retrieve her suitcase.

'Of course. I phoned her last night.' Premonition gripped her and she started to run towards the front door, fumbling in her bag for the key. But Keir was there beside her, taking the key from her fumbling fingers, gripping her arm as he pushed open the door and switched on the hall light.

'Gran!' Abigail called fearfully. 'Granny Lucy, where are you?'

A faint moan came from the kitchen and together they burst in. As Keir switched on the light the old lady sprawled on the floor moved feebly.

'No, don't try to move her,' Keir said as Abigail rushed in panic to her grandmother's side.

'But Keir, she's so cold!' Abigail chafed the old lady's icy hands. 'Darling, how long have you been lying here? Are you in pain?'

'Fetch some blankets and don't worry her with questions,' Keir ordered curtly. 'I'll phone for an ambulance.'

He took over, a tower of strength, and shocked into numb helplessness herself Abigail was glad of it, obediently climbing into the back of the ambulance to travel to the hospital with her grandmother and nodding gratefully when Keir said he would follow in his car when he had dropped Zena off at Marmion.

She was never more glad to see anyone when Keir

appeared at the door of that impersonal little waiting room, and tears welling in her eyes, the earlier unhappy rift between them forgotten, she threw herself into his arms.

'How is she? Have you see the doctor yet?' he asked when her tears were finally spent against his strong shoulder.

Abigail shook her head. 'No one's told me anything, but she seemed a lot better by the time we got here.' She managed a watery smile. 'She was even protesting that we were making a lot of fuss about nothing, bringing her in here.'

'It doesn't sound as if she's done much real damage then,' Keir said comfortingly.

And a short time later a doctor was confirming that optimistic diagnosis when he came to tell them there were no bones broken and that now she was warm again, the old lady had suffered no lasting harm, but he added that he thought it would be wise if they kept her in under observation overnight. If they telephoned first thing in the morning, they would probably be able to fetch her home tomorrow.

They were out in the car again when Abigail started to shake, her teeth chattering audibly. 'Delayed shock,' Keir pronounced, pulling her into the warmth and comfort of his arms. 'But you heard the doctor, honey. She's going to be all right.'

Abigail clung to him as the tremors stilled. 'I . . . I know,' she said shakily. 'But I can't help thinking what would have happened if I hadn't come home tonight——'

'But you *did* come home, and we found her in time,' he insisted, shaking her gently, coaxing her out of her morbid train of thought. 'Come on, what you need is a stiff drink.'

He drove her straight to Marmion and not even Zena's darting glance as she met them in the hall seemed to touch her.

'Ring through to the flat and ask Mrs Jameson if she'll pop over and get a room ready for Abigail,' Keir instructed his secretary. 'I'm not letting her stay in that house alone tonight. She'll sleep here. Perhaps you could loan her some nightwear, Zena, and Mrs Jameson will know where the spare toothbrushes are.'

'No need to disturb your housekeeper, I can see to all that,' Zena assured him quickly after asking about the old lady's condition, and while Keir took Abigail into the sitting room and thrust a glass of brandy into her hand, she went off, apparently all sympathy, to see to Abigail's comfort.

But it was Keir who took her up to her room when it was ready, glancing round to see that nothing had been missed, pushing her down on to the edge of the bed while he slipped off her shoes and leaning down to kiss her with restraint, admonishing her gently to have a good night's sleep, but adding wryly, 'Not that I expect to get much sleep myself.'

Emotionally exhausted and feeling the effects of the brandy, Keir's caring words echoing in her ears, Abigail fell almost immediately to sleep, only to wake again after a few hours. The illuminated clock at her bedside told her it was barely two o'clock and although the house was very still, sleep was suddenly out of reach. What might have happened to her beloved grandmother had Abigail *not* come home this particular weekend came back to haunt her. Of course she knew Granny Lucy was well into her seventies but finding her lying helpless as they had tonight brought home to her the old lady's frailty and vulnerability, living alone at Mill House.

She tossed and turned for the best part of half an hour then sighing she snapped on the bedside light and reached for the light robe Zena had loaned her along with the nightdress, experiencing a quiver of distaste as she shrugged it on and tied the girdle. The latch of her door clicked loudly in the stillness as she opened it but though a dim light still burned on the landing, nothing else stirred as she made her way to the bathroom.

She used the lavatory and washed her hands, then as she had hoped, found some aspirin in the bathroom cabinet and swallowed two down, trusting they would help to induce sleep. She had just emerged quietly from the bathroom when she saw Keir's door across the landing opening and her heart leapt. Perhaps he had heard her restlessness!

And then just as she stepped forward to apologise for waking him she stopped in stunned consternation. It wasn't Keir emerging from his room but Zena, and she was clad in only the filmiest of négligés that left nothing to the imagination. Rooted to the spot Abigail watched the other girl close Keir's bedroom door soundlessly behind her and turn, a small hand flying to her mouth as she caught sight of Abigail.

'Oh dear!' she said softly, casting a glance back at Keir's door as she moved away from it. 'I suppose this is what's called being caught in *flagrante delicto*!' She stretched sinuously, running her hands through her already tumbled, luxuriant auburn hair. 'You mustn't blame me too much, Abby dear. Keir's the most *fantastic* lover—as you'll find out for yourself soon— and I never could resist him.'

Abigail, through the mists of sick shock and searing pain, shook her head, trying to deny what she was seeing, what she was hearing. 'No! No, it's not true. Keir wouldn't—he *couldn't*——'

Zena laughed softly. 'Oh but he *could*. Haven't you learned yet he's incapable of remaining faithful to one woman? I accepted it long ago, which is why we're still together. Of course he's had other women in the last three years, but he always comes back to *me*.' With another gloating chuckle she strolled back to her own room.

Abigail stood where she was, incapable of moving. Even while he was planning their marriage, Keir was still continuing his intimate relations with his secretary! She could no longer pretend Zena's malicious innuendoes were merely to make trouble. They *were* lovers. Not even Abigail's own presence in the house tonight had deterred Keir from making the most of his mistress's availability. Sick hurt tore at her. No wonder he'd been so restrained in his goodnight kiss when he'd shown her to her room. No doubt he was already anticipating the more sophisticated pleasures he would find later with Zena. What was it he'd said? He didn't expect to sleep much himself tonight? And like a naive fool she'd believed that was because he'd be thinking about *her* being so close!

Her first impulse was to rush in on him, to confront him on that tumbled bed his mistress had only just vacated and tell him——

Tell him what? That their engagement was over now? That their marriage wouldn't be taking place after all? She shuddered violently. Could she really go in there and tell Keir everything was over between them? Did she really have the strength of mind and will to turn her back on her love for him, her overwhelming need of him, even though it was obvious his feelings for her were nowhere near as strong? And what other outcome could there possibly be if she confronted him now with what she knew?

Despising herself she turned and with slow, dragging footsteps went back to her own room to lie cold and sleepless through the darkest hours of the night. Oh God, if only she didn't love him so much! To never see him again, never respond to his lovemaking, to never know him fully as her body craved to do. It was more than she could bring herself to face. And yet how *could* she still love him, knowing him now for what he was, a heartless womaniser! Where was her pride?

The fact was that where Keir was concerned she didn't have any pride. She loved him. She wanted to marry him, spend the rest of her life with him. But she didn't want to share him.

'Oh why can't he love me as much as I love him?' she sobbed into her pillow. But he had never claimed to love her, had he? Oh many times he'd said he wanted her but never that he loved her.

What was left of that awful night was eventually banished by the dawn and the chorus of birdsong. Sounds downstairs heralded the arrival of Mrs Jameson to prepare their breakfast and as she dressed lethargically Abigail was no nearer seeing a way out of her agonising dilemma.

In spite of seeing the dawn break, Abigail was the last down to breakfast. Keir rose from the table as she hesitated in the dining-room doorway, trying to screw up her courage to face him, a shaft of pain at his duplicity stabbing her as his face lit up as if he was genuinely pleased to see her. But as his head came down to kiss her she was skin crawlingly aware of Zena's watchful, jealous eyes at the other side of the breakfast table, and she couldn't help herself shrinking away from him.

Frowning at her evasion of his kiss Keir followed the direction of her gaze and raised his eyebrows. 'Why so coy this morning?' His voice was only half teasing. 'Zena's seen me kiss you before and nothing's more certain than she'll see me doing it again.' He seemed to make an effort to throw off his irritation. 'Did you sleep well?'

How could he so carelessly kiss her in front of Zena, knowing what he and his secretary had shared last night? she wondered in hurt bewilderment. And how could he behave as if nothing had changed between him and herself? But of course he still didn't know that things had changed, did he? Not unless Zena had told him they had been found out, which seemed unlikely in view of his attitude.

She looked him straight in the eyes. 'No, I hardly slept at all as a matter of fact.'

Incredibly his expression softened. 'I'm sure you're worrying unnecessarily, darling. We'll call the hospital right after breakfast and I'm sure they'll tell you Granny Lucy's rarin' to go.'

'I'd rather phone from Mill House, Keir,' Abigail said quickly. 'That's if you can spare the time to run me home. Actually, I want to talk to you.' Her chin came up as she glanced at Zena. 'And I'd prefer to talk to you where I know we'll be alone.'

His searching eyes hadn't missed that involuntary glance at his secretary and they were suddenly expressionless, cool and grey as a winter sea, his nodded agreement curt.

Driving back to Mill House beside him, Abigail was acutely aware of his nearness and yet conscious that her request to go straight home had somehow distanced Keir from her. Her heart was beating heavily in her breast because even now she wasn't sure what she was going to say to him. She knew she was being pathetically weak-kneed but she wanted to avoid telling him she had actually *seen* Zena leaving his bed last night if she possibly could. To force him into admitting he and Zena were lovers would leave Abigail herself with no alternative but to end their engagement and that was something she couldn't bear to contemplate. Surely there had to be some way of touching his conscience without going to such lengths? Keir was basically a caring man, she was sure of that, and that deep down he did care about *her* she was equally sure. He had offered her marriage after all, something he hadn't offered to Zena.

Her mind was still whirling with half-formed opening gambits when she pushed open the front door of Mill House and saw her overnight bag still lying in the hall where she had dropped it the night before.

'Perhaps I should ring the hospital first,' she said, moving directly to the phone, unwilling to admit to herself she was putting off the moment of talking to

Keir. 'Would you like to make us some coffee?' she suggested with a forced smile.

'Well, how is she?' he demanded when a few minutes later she followed him into the kitchen.

'Granny Lucy's fine.' Abigail let out a long breath. At least that was one worry off her mind. 'They say I can fetch her home later on this morning.'

'Now having got that out of the way——' Keir pushed a mug of coffee across the table towards her, '—suppose you let me in on whatever it is that is imperative we be alone to talk about.'

He stood facing her across the table, very tall and dominant and heart-shakingly attractive, and all Abigail wanted to do was to throw herself into his arms and beg him to love her, to please love *only* her. Instead she made herself sit on one of the upright chairs and grasped the mug of coffee to steady her shaking hands. Now it came to her making her bid for his love and loyalty her mind was suddenly void of ideas that could bring it about.

'Well?' Keir's voice was harsh in the silence. 'Or is it suddenly not important to you any more?'

'Oh yes, it's important.' Abigail raised agonised eyes to his face. 'Keir, please don't expect me to share you with Zena after we're married.'

He drew in a hissing breath. 'Do you know what you're saying? You're asking me to sack the best secretary I ever had in order to pander to your petty jealousy! What else are you going to demand, I wonder?' His voice was dangerously angry in spite of its softness. 'That I give up my business interests and follow you around like a lap dog?'

Abigail ran her tongue round her dry lips. 'No, of course not. I——'

'You're dead right there, I'm not.' A few strides brought him round the table to tower over her, his coldly furious eyes making her shrink in her chair. 'I've tried to ignore your unreasonable jealousy of my secretary but this—this *request* of yours is not only insulting to both Zena and myself, it's sick.'

Sick? After last night? Abigail's hands were shaking so much the coffee slopped over them on to the table but she barely felt the sting of the hot liquid. 'Unreasonable! Are you trying to deny you and she are lovers, then?'

'Yes, I'm denying it.' He thrust his furious face close to hers. 'For your information, I don't risk losing a good secretary by complicating the issue with emotional entanglements. Neither have I so much as looked at another woman since I met you, much less lusted after one.'

He drew back, the tanned skin stretched tightly over his strong cheekbones, his eyes suddenly bleak as a dark frosty night. 'Not that I expect you to believe that. Jealousy like yours is an illness and doesn't respond to reason.'

'Keir, that's not true.' All thought of keeping her knowledge to herself was forgotten as she attempted to defend herself. 'I *know*——'

But he never gave her the chance, breaking in on her defence with a curt, 'Oh spare me any more of your wild imaginings.' He took a deep breath. 'No, Abigail, you won't have to share me with Zena after we're married because there isn't going to be any marriage.'

Everything seemed to whirl around her and her face blanched as she stared up at him, stricken. 'Keir. . . .' she whispered. 'You don't mean that!'

'I've never been more serious in my life.' His voice was suddenly weary though his expression was still as unyielding as granite. 'I've seen what obsessive jealousy like yours does to a marriage, Abigail, and no way am I going to put my head into *that* particular noose. I'm sorry, but it's over.' And incredibly he turned abruptly away from her and walked out.

At first Abigail was too stunned to move. By the time she did leap to her feet and rush to the door, his car was just disappearing out of the drive. Dropping on to the bottom stair she hugged her knees, staring disbelievingly into space. Keir had gone. Walked out of her life.

How had it happened? Fragments of what he had said echoed in her brain. '... you won't have to share me with Zena after we're married because there isn't going to be a marriage ... sorry, but it's over ... I've seen what obsessive jealousy like yours does to a marriage. ...'

Accusing her when *he* was the guilty one! Keir had been the one to break their engagement when it was *she* who had the real justification. She rocked herself to and fro in an agony of loss. Did it matter who had made the break? She had lost him and she wanted to die!

Time slid by unnoticed as she huddled there at the bottom of the stairs, trying to make sense of this catastrophe that had fallen on her so utterly unexpectedly from the sky. It was the grandfather clock striking eleven that brought the reminder through her haze of pain that though it felt as if her life had ended, her grandmother was waiting to be collected from the hospital.

Obsessive jealousy! Keir's totally unjust accusation pierced her like a knife as she collected her car keys and backed her Mini out to drive into the city. Hadn't he given her good reason to be jealous? All right, so he didn't know she had seen Zena leaving his room last night, but his own conscience must tell him her jealousy was *not* unfounded as she had claimed.

Her grandmother was in high spirits, demanding to know at once where Keir was and why he hadn't come with Abigail. Hurting too rawly to talk about it yet, Abigail made the excuse that he was busy. Her ring still winked brightly on her finger—Keir must have forgotten to ask for its return—so at least she could keep up the pretence of her engagement until she had come to terms with the fact of having to live the rest of her life without him. If she ever did ....

Settling her grandmother in a chair in a sheltered corner of the garden well wrapped up in rugs after a lunch Abigail herself had only been able to pick at, she wandered back into the house, her hand reaching involuntarily for the telephone. Fumbling, she dialled the number of Marmion, not knowing what she would say when he answered, only knowing she couldn't accept yet that everything was over between them. But there was no reply.

Later that evening and several times on Sunday she dialled both Marmion and Keir's apartment in London, but each time the phone rang and rang endlessly.

It took the courage of desperation to ring through to his office on Monday morning, and of course this time her call was answered.

'Abigail!' Zena's surprise when she asked to speak to Keir told her the other girl knew of the rift between them. 'Abigail, you must know——'

'Oh yes, I'm sure he's told you our engagement's off,' she broke in bitterly. 'And I wouldn't be ringing him now if it wasn't important.' Well it was important, wasn't it, to any hope of salvaging her future? 'Please, Zena.' It cost her pride a lot to beg her rival to allow her access to Keir. 'I *must* speak to him. I promise I won't take up much of his time.'

There was a lengthy silence at the other end but at last Zena said unwillingly, 'Just a minute, I'll go and see. . . .' Another wait, much longer this time, and Abigail's heart plunged when it was Zena's voice back on the line. 'He's too busy to speak to you now,' Zena said briskly. 'He's got things to do before he leaves for Wales. But he says if it's that important he'll break his journey. Not that he's got any time to waste, mind, but if you'll meet him in that layby on the Newton Road about a mile outside Great Wiston, he'll give you a few minutes.'

A few minutes by the side of the road, Abigail thought despairingly, but however unpromising it sounded, she grasped the chance of seeing him again eagerly.

CHAPTER SIX

'YOU'RE never working already, Miss Abigail!' There was reproof in Mrs Price's voice as Serge's kindly housekeeper came into her room after a brisk knock. 'You'll wear yourself to a shadow if you go on like this. Come on, now, get some of this hot tea inside you.'

Abigail put aside the manuscript she had been working on and easing her cramped limbs, accepted the cup with grateful thanks. She didn't tell Mrs Price she had been working all night wrapped up in the quilt, huddled against the padded headboard of the bed, afraid to sleep, knowing the dreadful nightmares that had haunted her for so long after her discharge from hospital were lying in wait for her if she closed her eyes, sparked off by the shock of meeting Keir again. Only so far had she allowed the memories of him to be disinterred and no farther, even now not able to bear the pain of remembering his final, brutal betrayal. So she had worked doggedly through what was left of the night to keep all thought of him out of her mind.

But now, her eyes gritty, her head heavy from lack of sleep, the threat of his presence in London came rushing back, destroying her hard-won sense of security, demolishing her fragile peace of mind. Keir was here. He had deliberately sought her out last night, obviously attending her benefit concert because he knew she would be there. Serge's quiet little house in Chelsea was no longer the safe haven she had thought it when Keir's London apartment was less than a mile away.

If only she hadn't let Serge talk her into this visit to London! If only she could get on the first available train back to the safe anonymity of her cottage. But there was her appointment with her music publisher this morning.

She knew her old friend's perceptive gaze was noting her dark-circled eyes and trembling tension when she joined him for breakfast. 'My dear! You didn't sleep well last night?' he demanded in concern.

Abigail shook her head, knowing it was useless to deny it when she looked such a wreck.

'But you're surely not worried about your appointment this morning? You know your publisher's been waiting eagerly for your new collection of studies for students.'

Abigail shook her head again, glancing in dismay at the piled plate Mrs Price put before her and expected her to eat. 'It . . . it's not that.' She fitted her fork into her damaged hand and toyed with some of the scrambled egg.

'Then what is it?' Serge pressed gently.

'It . . . it's Keir.' The words were wrung out of her with difficulty and she raised dark frantically anxious eyes. 'I . . . I'm so afraid of running into him again.'

'Your one-time fiancé? It upset you so much, seeing him again?' Serge couldn't hide his surprise but then he laughed at her gently. 'And do you really imagine that with all the millions of people in London you're likely to so much as catch a glimpse of him on your way to your appointment?'

Put like that her fear did seem unreasonable. 'I suppose not,' she admitted in a low voice. And yet what did *reason* have to do with any of Keir's actions? 'I just wish I could get on the next train back home,' she blurted desperately. 'I shan't feel safe again until I close my own front door behind me.'

'Safe?' Serge's bushy eyebrows rose. 'My dear, don't you think you're being a bit melodramatic? I can understand that meeting the man you once loved might have given you an unpleasant shock but why should it make you feel unsafe? As I pointed out, the chances of running into him accidentally again must be several million to one, and as you made it blisteringly clear to him last night you had no more time for him, he's hardly likely to risk bruising his ego again by seeking you out, is he?'

'You don't understand. . . .' Pushing her plate away she rested her elbows on the table and buried her face in her hands. How could she explain to Serge her conviction that Keir's presence at the concert last night had been no accident? How could she admit she had very good cause to be afraid of the man she had once loved so much, and that nothing she could say would bruise his ego enough to deter him from hunting her down if it suited his purpose? She had never told a soul what Keir had done to her a year ago, had even imagined some of the emotional scars had healed along with the physical ones. But seeing him again last night had torn the tender tissue to reveal a still-festering wound.

'How can I understand when you won't tell me what it is that's eating away at you?' Serge said gently. He had risen from his seat and come round the table to put a comforting arm around her thin shoulders. 'The thing that's been eating at you ever since your accident.'

Fear, bewilderment and sheer weariness tempted her to share with him the terrible secret she had kept to herself for so long, but even while her brain formed the words, her tongue refused to utter them.

Serge sighed at the prolonged silence. 'Abigail, you're not going to conquer your irrational fears by running away from them,' he said at last. 'But if it makes you feel any easier about going out today, then I'll come with you. We can take a taxi from door to door.'

If only her fears *were* irrational, Abigail thought. The only irrational thing about the whole business was the reason Keir had for seeking her destruction. She looked up at her old friend, her eyes full of gratitude. 'Thank

you, Serge. You're very good to me. . . .' Her voice
choked.

He patted her shoulder. 'Nonsense, my dear. What's
a little thing like giving up my morning when you know
I would give all I have to see you restored to the happy
young woman you once were?'

By the time Serge was flagging down a cab for the
return trip to Chelsea, Abigail was prepared to admit
that perhaps her fears about this outing to her
publishers *had* been foolish. The journey by taxi across
London had been slow but uneventful – no avenging
demon had fallen on her from the skies, no bogeyman
had leapt upon her round a corner – and her reception
by Mr Bowers, whom she had only corresponded with
before, had been flatteringly cordial.

He had made much of her, immediately looking
over the work she had brought with her and declaring
it to be just what he'd been hoping for, and
congratulating her on the reception her first serious
piece of music had received at the concert the
previous evening, expressing the hope that now it had
been performed in public by such an eminent
exponent as Ling Tan, demand for copies of the work
would grow. He enthused over how well her earlier
collection of elementary studies for students was
selling before going on to invite her to do a third
collection for them to complete the series.

The only jarring note was struck when Mr Bowers
said, 'You know Miss Paston, I can't understand why
you didn't take up teaching when your career as a
performer came to such an untimely end. Someone of
your experience and talent has such a lot to give, and
you seem to know instinctively how to introduce your
students to new techniques.'

'I *do* teach, Mr Bowers.' Abigail was immediately on
the defensive. 'Two days a week I give lessons at a
preparatory school not far from where I live and I also
have a few pupils who come to my home. Not many, I

admit. The cottage is a bit isolated from the village for some parents to let their children trail up there.'

'My dear Miss Paston, I'm not talking about teaching farmers' daughters to tinkle a few tunes!' Mr Bowers sounded quite offended at the idea. 'I'm talking of you teaching serious students. I'm sure any reputable college of music would jump at the chance of having you on their faculty. Don't you agree, Mr Markovitch?' He appealed to Serge for support.

'Indeed I do,' the elderly teacher agreed. 'I've never liked her burying herself in that run-down cottage of hers.'

But Abigail was shaking her head vehemently. 'I couldn't live in London again, Mr Bowers.' Especially not now she knew Keir was living here again, she added to herself with an inward shudder.

The publisher seemed about to argue the point but something in Serge's expression must have warned him off for he said instead, 'Well of course teaching would leave you less time for writing your own music. Now your first piece has been launched, do you have plans for something to follow it up?'

Abigail admitted she had. 'As a matter of fact I've been working on something in sonata form,' she said diffidently.

Mr Bower's eyebrows rose. 'Ambitious!'

Abigail flushed. Too ambitious? She back-tracked at once. 'Of course the ideas are only fragmentary as yet, and I don't suppose anything will come of them.'

'Well if you ever do complete it – and if it comes up to the standard of your prelude – I'm sure we'd be interested to see it,' Mr Bowers said.

Her flush deepened. Was he being patronising? She couldn't help remembering Serge's confession that he had manipulated Mr Bowers into publishing her prelude when he might not otherwise have been interested. Raphael Andre's criticism last night that her work lacked inner fire and feeling still stuck like a thorn in her flesh. The idea that her prelude had been published and performed for any other reason than the merit of the work struck at the foundations of her shaky self-esteem. And yet Ling Tan *had* had enough faith in its worth to perform it. Unless he too had only included it in his programme out of pity for a fellow performer who had fallen on hard times?

That was something else Keir Minto had done to her, she thought bitterly, not only destroying her career as a performer, but destroying her faith in herself as a woman and as an artist too.

'Unless I feel the sonata *surpasses* the standard of the prelude, it won't be offered for publication, Mr Bowers,' she said stiffly.

'Spoken like the true professional you are, Miss Paston.' Mr Bowers' smile of approval went a small way towards banishing her doubts about herself. 'And if it does surpass the prelude, you'll have performers of the calibre of Ling Tan queuing up to play it.'

'You didn't tell me you were planning a sonata, Abigail,' Serge said when they were settled in the back of the taxi cab for the run back to Chelsea, and with a swift thrust of compunction Abigail realised he was hurt that he hadn't been the first to know.

'I'm sorry, Serge.' She took his hand and squeezed it. 'I don't know what made me blurt it out like that, and I regretted it as soon as I'd opened my mouth. You know I never like to talk about my work until I've got something down on paper. Discussing it too soon dissipates the creative energy somehow, and as I said, the ideas are still only fragmentary.' And yet she knew with a deep conviction that the music was there inside her. She could feel it forming, stirring, shifting, hear odd phrases with her inner ear. All she needed was the key to unlock the door.

'Ah, the gestation period.' Serge nodded his understanding and promptly began to talk about something else until the cab drew up outside his front door.

They had reached the top of the flight of stairs to the first floor when Mrs Price came bustling out of her kitchen at the back of the house. 'You have a visitor,' she called up to them.

'In the music room?' Serge began at once to retrace his steps while Abigail continued on. She was actually pushing open the sitting-room door when Mrs Price said cheerfully, 'No, I put him in the sitting room. It's someone to see Miss Abigail.'

Her eyes dilated and the now familiar cold sweat of panic beaded her upper lip and brow as Keir rose slowly from an easy chair beside the fire. She wanted to turn and run but the sheer weight of her terror held her immobile.

'Abby, for God's sake stop looking at me as if I frighten the living daylights out of you!' he burst out harshly, and Abigail began to shake.

'For some reason, apparently you do, Mr Minto,' Serge's voice said quietly behind her, his arm coming protectively round her trembling shoulders. 'Come, Abigail, sit down before you fall down,' he coaxed, and though she tried to resist she didn't have the strength. She slumped into the corner of the sofa and huddled there, trying to control her tremors.

Standing protectively over her, Serge turned to their visitor. 'Now Mr Minto, I'm sure you can see Abigail doesn't find this visit welcome so perhaps you will state your business.'

'I have no wish to frighten her. I only want to talk to her.' Keir's voice sounded strained. 'And I would prefer to do it privately.'

Just as she was getting it under control, the panic welled up again as Serge looked at her questioningly. 'No! Please Serge, don't go. I don't know how he followed me here or what he wants but there's nothing I have to say to him.'

'Lady Elizabeth told me I'd find you here with your friend and protector.' That last word had a jibing note and there was hard anger in his face as he went on, 'And after the veiled accusations you made last night implying that you hold *me* responsible for the accident that finished your career, I think you owe me an explanation.'

Abigail stared at him incredulously. 'You want to talk about *that*?'

His eyes narrowed. 'I want to talk about that,' he agreed flatly. 'When someone flings an unfounded accusation like that at me I think I have the right to know why.'

Abigail gasped. 'Unfounded!' Her head whirled as she tried to make sense of his motive for coming here, for forcing the terrible thing he had done into the open. She took a deep breath and from somewhere found the courage to look at him steadily. 'I assured you last night I've never told anyone what really happened that day, not the police, not my grandmother, not Serge. Do you really want to drag it all into the light of day now?'

'Yes, damn you, then perhaps I'll be able to understand why you cringe away from me as if I was a beast with two heads.'

Abigail shuddered. 'Then Serge stays and hears too.' She looked up pleadingly at her old friend. 'For my own protection, he stays.'

Serge looked questioningly at her and then at the younger man and when Keir merely shrugged, he sat down on the sofa beside her.

Her damaged hand covered with the black glove she always wore to hide the scars ached abominably and she massaged it as she began with painful reluctance, 'I . . . I told the police when they questioned me in hospital that I didn't recognise the other car involved. It . . . it wasn't true.' She lifted huge, pain-filled eyes to the man standing before the fireplace. 'I knew the car very well. It was Keir's black Porsche.'

The appalling memory she had kept buried for twelve months was as clear and as terrifying as if it was happening now. 'He was parked in the layby where we'd arranged to meet. He waited till I stopped and got out of my car and then he deliberately drove straight at me. I leapt back, flattening myself against the Mini, but I'd left the door wide open. His car hit it at speed and slammed it shut on my hand. And then he drove off.'

'My dearest child!'

But Abigail hardly heard Serge's shocked ejaculation as she watched Keir's face drain to a dirty grey beneath his tan.

'You bitch!' he snarled, and sprang at her.

Abigail cowered back against the cushions, knowing herself helpless in the face of his attack. He seized first one arm and then the other, roughly pushing up the sleeves of her sweater and examining the inner sides of her elbows. And before Serge could struggle protesting to his feet he had already contemptuously released her and stepped back.

'It's all right, I was only looking for signs of drug addiction,' he said cruelly. 'There has to be *some* explanation for this fantastic lie. Tell me, Abigail, exactly when was this murderous assault supposed to have taken place?'

Abigail pulled down her sleeves to cover the red marks his rough handling had left on her arms that tomorrow would be bruises. But what were a few bruises, she thought wildly, after what he had already done? 'You know when.' Her voice was an anguished thread of sound. 'The Monday morning after you broke off our engagement.'

'Two days *after*.' His voice was flat but it suddenly crackled with contempt. 'You really should have taken the trouble to ascertain your facts, Abigail, before weaving such tall stories. When I left you at Mill House after breaking the engagement I drove straight to London and caught the first standby flight for Canada. By the time our unlikely tryst was supposed to be taking place I was in a logging camp in northern

Manitoba. And if your accident happened when you said it did, how do you explain that a few weeks later you were off on tour again? Oh yes,' he jeered at her startled jerk, 'I might have put as much distance between us as possible but I still couldn't help being concerned about you so I had someone keep me informed. I also know,' he added savagely, 'that when you came back to London after that tour, you immediately moved in with another man.'

Abigail could only stare at him in dumb bewilderment. Had he sought her out, insisted on her exposing him before a witness just so he could deny all involvement in her injury? It was her word against his now, she realised impotently. She had said nothing to the police at the time so would they be likely to believe her now if she accused him? She thought it was unlikely. But why, having denied her account of *how* her injury happened, was he now accusing her of lying about *when* it happened? And why make the ridiculous allegation of her going to live with another man? After her sleepless night her tired brain could make no sense of his motives.

'This is dreadful ... dreadful. ...' Serge muttered beside her. 'But at least one thing can be established without question.' He got unsteadily to his feet and crossed to the bookcase where he drew out a heavy volume. As he opened it Abigail saw it was the scrapbook containing press cuttings relating to her own career. From the back of the book he took a folded sheet of newspaper.

'I kept this, the *finis* of my protégé's career, but somehow I could never bring myself to cut out the item and stick it in the book,' Serge said sadly. He opened out the sheet of newspaper and held it out to Keir, pointing out the paragraph. 'You see the newspaper carries the date, Mr Minto.'

Abigail watched as Keir frowningly read the report that a hit-and-run driver had put an end to the career of the young concert pianist Abigail Paston, and saw the furrow between his brows deepen as his eyes flicked to the date at the top of the page. 'But this was weeks before——'

'Before what Mr Minto?' Serge prompted.

Keir looked up, a dazed expression on his face. 'Before I was told Abigail was off on another concert tour, her career going from strength to strength.'

'I can assure you Abigail was in no condition to go on any tour,' Serge said dryly. 'She was in hospital for eight weeks and the only man she ever lived with was me. I brought her here when the hospital discharged her as her grandmother was too unwell to look after her. Mrs Paston suffered a heart attack—brought on by the shock of Abigail's accident—and died a short time later.'

'My God! Abby. . . .' Keir's face was drained with shock, his eyes appalled. Abigail had never seen him look so shaken and she frowned her own puzzlement because it appeared so genuine.

'Might I ask who told you that palpably untrue account of Abigail's continued career?' Serge carefully refolded the page of newspaper and replaced it in the scrapbook.

'My . . . my secretary,' Keir said in a low voice.

'Zena!' The name came out on a hissed breath as Abigail stiffened rigidly.

Again she seemed to see the woman Keir had betrayed her with, her green eyes mocking, her luxuriant hair tumbled, coming out of his room at Marmion in the early hours of the morning.

She could actually taste the bitterness in her mouth as she flung at him now, 'And there could be no possible reason why your utterly fascinating, utterly indispensable mistress should make up a tale of me going on tour and taking a lover, could there Keir? Or perhaps you both concocted it together.'

'This woman was your mistress?' Serge broke in sharply.

'No!' Keir's denial was explosive. 'Though for some reason Abigail had convinced herself she was. That was what broke us up, her obsessive jealousy of Zena. I just couldn't take any more.'

'For pity's sake!' Abigail didn't think she could stand much more of this raking over of the past, this raising of emotions she had thought long buried and wanted to stay that way. Like a puppet on a string she sprang to her feet and moved jerkily to the window. 'Why bother to go on denying it, Keir? Zena never did. She got quite a lot of pleasure out of telling me you were lovers—even boasting about it—and how you'd never give her up even if you were fool enough to marry me.' She could still hear Zena's gloating voice, 'Haven't you learned yet that Keir's incapable of remaining faithful to one woman? I accepted it long ago, which is why we're still together. Of course he's had other women in the last three years, but he always comes back to *me*.'

'Then she was lying,' Keir said harshly.

'That's what I thought at first. I couldn't bring myself to believe——' Her voice choked and she spun round to face him with the passionate accusation, 'So how do you explain that every time I phoned you from Germany it was always Zena who answered the call? However late at night it was and whether I rang you at your apartment in London or at Marmion, she was always there, laughing at me?'

'She was my *secretary*. While you were away I filled in the time working long hours and she never objected.' But his anger sounded forced, as if for the first time he wasn't sure of his ground.

'Oh I'm sure she didn't object,' Abigail said scornfully. 'And was she "working" that night at Marmion when they kept Granny Lucy in hospital after her fall? Too bad I couldn't sleep and had to get up to go to the bathroom in the early hours. Only Zena wasn't a bit put out when I saw her leaving your room.

In fact she flaunted it in my face, what a fantastic and irresistible lover you were.'

'You *saw* her leaving my room!' Abigail had hardly taken in his apparent incredulity before he was striding across the room, gripping her thin shoulders and shaking her. 'For God's sake, if you felt you had some basis for your suspicions about my relationship with Zena, why didn't you tell me?'

'Mr Minto!' Serge protested but Keir ignored him.

His fingers bit painfully against her bones, but worse than that, the control over her emotions she had struggled so assiduously to build up over the last twelve months was gone and she hurt all over. 'Because I *loved* you!' she screamed at him. 'I didn't *want* you to confirm everything Zena told me. I just wanted it to stop.'

Keir groaned and his agonising grip on her shoulders relaxed, gentling to a caress, moving with a remembered sensuality. Even through the thickness of her sweater Abigail's skin tingled at his touch, her nerve ends suddenly sensitised, a responding warmth curling in the pit of her stomach.

Even now, after all he had made her suffer, he could still work his old magic! Abigail was appalled at herself and twisted violently away from him.

'You say you loved me, and yet you could still believe I'd deliberately run you down?' He moved his broad shoulders as if they were carrying an unbearable weight. 'Why in heaven would I want to do such a barbarous thing?'

Abigail moaned. 'Don't you think I asked myself that a million times? I only know I have to believe the evidence of my own eyes. It was *your* car, Keir, waiting in the layby where you'd arranged to meet me.'

'I told you,' he said wearily. 'I was already in Canada by then, so how could I have arranged a meeting with you, much less have been there? You're surely not claiming you spoke to me again after I left Mill House that day?'

'No. I rang your office but Zena said you were much too busy to talk to me,' she said bitterly, feeling again the humiliation of having to plead with Keir through his mistress. 'But when I insisted it was important that I see you, she kindly reported back that you'd spare me a few minutes of your time if I'd meet you on that layby in Newton Road.'

He shook his head. 'I don't understand any of this. Why would Zena say I'd be there when she knew very well I was already in Canada? Unless——' His eyes narrowed.

'Unless I've made the whole thing up, is that what you're trying to imply? That the whole thing is a figment of my imagination?' She felt very close to the edge of hysteria at his persistence in clinging to the weak alibi that he'd been in Canada and nowhere near Newton Lane that day. 'Tell me I've imagined this, then!' Peeling off her black glove and not caring how much the removal hurt, she stuck her left hand under his nose.

'Oh God!' The colour drained out of his face leaving it greenish and sickly as he stared in horrified fascination at the scarred and stiff travesty of what had once been a strong, supple hand. The sight of it seemed to have at last brought home to him the enormity of what he had done and Abigail was glad.

'Not very pretty, is it?' she taunted, wanting to hurt him as she had been hurt. 'But no figment of my imagination any more than the car lying in wait for me in that layby was. *Your* car Keir, your black Porsche with the tinted windows and the personalised number plate—KM 100.'

There was a chinking of glass at the sideboard and a moment later Serge pushed a brandy glass into Keir's hand and urged him back into a chair. He offered no resistance and after taking a sip, raised tormented eyes to Abigail's face. 'Abby, if it *was* my car, I swear to you it wasn't me driving it. You surely can't really believe I'd do such a terrible and senseless thing?'

Dear God but he was a superlative actor to still be able to deny his responsibility and to look like a man on the rack while he did it! He almost had her believing him, almost had her feeling sorry for him. She hardened her heart. When had Keir ever shown pity for her?

'Do you think I *wanted* to believe it, even with the evidence of my own eyes?' she said raggedly. 'I nearly went quietly out of my mind, lying there in hospital all those weeks remembering every detail.'

Serge's arm came protectively round her waist and she turned her face into his shoulder to hide the threatened tears. 'My dear,' he said hesitantly, 'can you be absolutely sure it *was* Keir driving that car? You did say it had tinted windows.'

It was a measure of Keir's personality that even Serge could doubt his guilt. 'Oh yes, I'm sure. Even though it happened so quickly and I couldn't see clearly through the tinted glass, I'm very sure.' She turned from the old man's troubled face to meet Keir's eyes. 'You shouldn't have worn that high-crowned lumber jack's cap, Keir, to pull down over your face. They might be common enough in Canada but the shape and style is very distinctive here.'

Keir's gaze was the first to drop and his head bowed, she thought in defeat. She ought to feel pleased to see that arrogant self-confidence brought low, she thought, but she could feel no satisfaction, only an empty, soul-crushing weariness. She turned away from him only to spin back when Keir said fiercely, 'I wish to God you'd told the police your suspicions at the time, then at least I'd have been given the chance to establish my innocence. Why didn't you, Abigail, when you were so convinced of my guilt?'

'I . . . couldn't.' She felt as if she was crumbling inside. Tears filled her eyes and poured silently down her cheeks, tears she had been too deeply shocked to shed a year ago, welling up out of a bottomless pit of pain and disillusion. 'I just wanted to die. . . .'

'Abigail, my dearest girl.' Serge clucked around her, helpless in the face of her deep distress. 'Mr Minto, I think you should go now. This child's on the point of collapse.'

The man who sprang out of the chair and stood over her bore little resemblance to the man who a few minutes ago had looked so defeated. All the forceful confidence was back, threatening, dangerous.

'All right, I'll leave,' he said tightly. 'But I'll be back.'

CHAPTER SEVEN

'You heard him. He said he'd be back!'

The sound of the front door closing behind Keir had acted like a starting gun and Abigail had raced up the second flight of stairs to her room. By the time the protesting Serge had caught up with her, she was flinging her clothes haphazardly into her suitcase.

'Abigail, my dear child, you can't rush away like this,' he remonstrated worriedly. 'You're hysterical, in no fit state to travel back to that cottage alone.'

'I must.' She swept up the toilet articles on the dressing table and dropped them on top of her clothes. 'I can't stay here, not now Keir knows where to find me. You must see that.'

Serge dropped on to the edge of the bed, his breathing laboured after hurrying up the stairs. 'I know he said he'd be back, but it won't be today. Probably not tomorrow either. That was a very shaken man who left here, Abigail.'

She frowned, her hands clumsily struggling to fasten her suitcase suddenly still. Keir *had* been shaken when brought face to face with the enormity of what he'd done to her. Shaken, but hardly remorseful, she reminded herself. He'd still persisted in denying it and his final words had been threatening.

She raised wide, frightened eyes to her old friend. 'You believed his story, then? That he was somewhere in the wilds of Canada and *not* driving that car?'

Serge shook his head. 'My dear, I don't know what to believe, but it was plain to me your accusation shocked him. I'd swear it was utterly unexpected.'

Abigail's mouth twisted bitterly. She couldn't deny that Keir had put on a very convincing performance even if his alibi was pathetically weak. But then he'd once managed to convince her he loved her. She'd been taken in by him once herself, so perhaps she shouldn't blame Serge too much for being taken in by him now. It was frightening though, to know Keir had managed to turn her only friend against her and it made her feel terribly alone and vulnerable.

'So you think I'm lying, making it all up?'

'No!' Serge looked shocked. 'My dear girl, I know *you* believe he was driving that car, and I must admit from what you said the evidence seems conclusive. But couldn't there be the remotest chance that you were mistaken?'

If only there was that chance. . . . She pushed that yearning thought down ruthlessly because it disturbed emotions she didn't want stirred again. 'Serge, I *know* what happened. Why else did I nearly go out of my mind?'

The old man sighed heavily. 'Yes, I always knew there was something more than the pain and the loss of your career that was preying on your mind.' He sighed again. 'What a terrible knowledge you kept to yourself! No wonder you were so afraid of him.' The silence stretched out as Abigail managed to get her case fastened. 'You think he still wants to harm you?'

'I don't know.' And yet what other reason could Keir have for coming back into her life? Glancing at Serge she was glad she hadn't voiced that thought aloud. He seemed to have shrunk. It was no longer her champion and mentor sitting there on the edge of the bed but a helpless old man and he looked ill. She felt a swift compunction at having involved him in the confrontation with Keir and hastened to assure him, 'No, I hardly think he'd risk it, do you? He must be aware now that any other "accident" befalling me would make you suspect him at once.'

'So there's really no need for you to rush off at once back to the cottage, is there?' he appealed.

Abigail shivered. Maybe her physical terror of Keir had receded but she was still afraid of him. Or was it herself she was afraid of? She couldn't get out of her mind the memory of that moment when his punishing grip had turned to a caress and her body's instinctive response. After all that had happened she was appalled that he should still have the power to make her feel like that when she should have been cowering away in revulsion.

She crossed to the bed and squeezed her old friend's hands, making an effort to keep her voice calm and even to reassure him. 'I don't know what Keir hopes to gain by coming here again but I'd really rather not stay around to find out. Serge, for *your* sake as much as my own you must see it would be better to avoid any more painful scenes like this morning's. I'm perfectly all right now, I promise you, and I'll feel even better when I'm back home and safely out of his way.'

Serge nodded. 'You're probably right, my dear,' he said sadly. 'But I had such high hopes of this visit. I hoped that meeting your old friends and colleagues again would draw you back into the musical world where you belong, but here you are, scuttling back to that cottage—and even more determined not to leave it again.'

Abigail couldn't help feeling guilty, knowing how much the old man worried about her. 'Serge, please don't think I'm ungrateful for all you've done for me—the introduction to Mr Bowers, the concert, getting my music performed. I'll never be able to thank you enough for all your support and encouragement. But I'm happy in my little cottage, you must believe that.'

That assertion came back to her three hours later as she paid off the taxi that had brought her from the station and let the stillness enfold her as she shut the cottage door on the outside world. Happy? Well there was no harm in letting Serge believe so, even though she knew that what she found here wasn't even contentment, more an absence of feeling. The constant hum of traffic along the main road at the bottom of the lane only intensified the sense of being cut off from the mainstream, sheltered, safe from destróying emotion.

Dodie's Retreat was a row of four adjoining cottages and Abigail's was the last one. In front of the cottages where once had been long individual strips of garden it was now one large lawn kept regularly mowed by the trustees, but the door leading out to it from the front parlour had long ago ceased to open from disuse. The only entrance to the cottage now was at the back where a row of outhouses—coal stores and lavatories—faced the back doors across a communal yard.

Inside it was cold and smelled faintly musty after being shut up for three days. Compared to the solid comfort of Serge's home it was distinctly shabby. The original stone sink had at some time been replaced by an enamelled unit but earlier, careless tenants had chipped it badly. Smoke and steam had streaked the yellow colour-washed walls to brown over the old-fashioned cooking range and although the colours of the thick rug she had brought with her from her grandmother's home were still bright, the linoleum covering the rest of the floor looked even more worn by contrast. The recesses either side of the fireplace were filled in by floor-to-ceiling cupboards, their doors ill-fitting and warped with age. The easy chair to one side of the range with its faded chintz loose cover looked at home in its setting but the small formica topped table and two vinyl-covered chairs—only one of which was ever used—looked incongruously modern, and beside it the big, out-of-date refrigerator she had brought with her from Mill House took up far too much space.

But at least there was nothing here to remind her of Keir Minto. She was able to leave all memories of him, both past and now recent, on the other side of the door. Putting down her suitcase she collected newspaper and kindling and began the delicate and frustrating operation of relighting the fire in the range, and when it

was finally going, opening the door into the tiny
parlour to let the air circulate as it warmed up to keep
the damp out of the upright piano on which she
instructed her pupils.

She carried her suitcase upstairs, pausing to wash her
grubby hands in the spartan bathroom, before
unpacking. The bedroom came nearest to her old room
at Mill House, having her own bed with its brass-railed
head and pretty flower-sprigged cover, the matching
brass-trimmed bedside table and the lamp with the
pleated silk shade her grandmother had made. The
warm rug to protect her bare feet from the chill of cold
linoleum had come from her old room too, but the
dressing table and small wardrobe—all that could be
squeezed into the limited space—had come from one of
her grandmother's spare rooms, and although the
curtains matched the sprigged bedcover, they were
much too big for the small window, for with the use of
only hand Abigail had been unable to undertake the
task of altering them to fit.

She unpacked then went down to the kitchen,
removing the thin layer of dust that had coated every
surface in her absence while she waited for the fire to
glow, then heated up a can of soup which she ate with
crackers and some rather stale cheese. Making out a
shopping list to replenish her larder took up some more
time until the water was hot enough for a bath, and by
eight o'clock she was ready to tumble into bed, worn
out by the strain of being the cynosure of all eyes at the
concert the night before followed by the shock of seeing
Keir again and her sleepless night, and by the sheer
effort of burying the memory of her confrontation with
him that morning deep in her subconscious mind where
it could no longer touch her.

She slept at once but woke in the morning feeling
unrefreshed, as if her dreams had been uneasy and
frightening even if she couldn't remember them.

Slowly the uneventfulness of her days relaxed her as

she slid back into her routine, washing her clothes at
the kitchen sink and drying them on a line strung
between the cottage and the outhouse, carrying coal in
her daily battle to keep the reluctant range alight,
shopping in the village on her way back from her twice-
weekly stint as music teacher at the prep school, trying
to instil her own love of music into the often reluctant
pupils who came to her cottage for lessons.

The university term had started again and the student
occupants had returned to the other cottages so
crossing to the coal store to refill her bucket one
morning almost a week after her precipitate return from
London, she didn't immediately take any notice of the
tall man walking up the yard. It was only as he came on
that her skin started to prickle and she turned her head
sharply like an animal scenting danger, and though the
surge of adrenalin urged her to flight, the sight of Keir
Minto moving implacably towards her took all the use
from her legs.

'H . . . how did you find me?' she croaked. Not that it
really mattered now. She should have known he would
hunt her down somehow.

But she found it did matter when he said, 'Serge
Markovitch told me.'

She raised wounded eyes to his face. Never for one
moment had she thought Serge might betray her.

'He told me because he knows I don't want to hurt
you.' There was a sudden savagery in his voice when he
added, 'God knows you've already been hurt enough!'

Abigail's shoulders drooped in defeat, a curious
fatalism overtaking her so that she hardly noticed when
the empty bucket banged against her leg. Keir took it
from her. 'What were you going to do with this?'

She indicated the coal store without speaking,
watching him as he opened the door and began to fill
the bucket. It was only as he emerged that she realised
she had missed her chance of running back to the
cottage and locking herself in. Now he was immediately

behind her and it was too late. It would only have postponed the inevitable anyway.

He followed her inside, putting the bucket down in the hearth and straightening to survey the cramped, primitive kitchen. 'You've been living *here* for twelve months!'

The tone of his voice reduced her home to a hovel and she was stung into retaliating, 'I've only been slumming it for nine months, actually. I was in hospital for eight weeks don't forget, and after that with Serge for a while. Then I came back to live at Mill House until Granny Lucy died and I couldn't afford to stay there any more. I know this isn't what *you're* used to but it was the best I could do since you left me with no means of providing myself with anything better.'

His face whitened and he seemed to flinch. 'Last week I gained the impression you lived permanently with Mr Markovitch.'

'That would have salved your conscience, would it?' His presence seemed to fill every corner of the small room, underlining the fact that this place would never be a safe haven for her again. But the reminder of her old teacher brought a shaft of anxiety. 'Just what did you do to Serge to persuade him to tell you where to find me? I can't believe he would have given me away voluntarily.'

For all the ruthless determination emanating from him Keir's expression was oddly uncertain, pleading. 'I talked to him—as I hope to talk to you.' He reached into his inside pocket and drew out an envelope which he held out to her. 'Perhaps this'll convince you I'm on the level and didn't have to use thumb screws to get your whereabouts out of him.'

As she reached out to take the letter Abigail recognised at once Serge's elaborate, spidery script. Apprehensively she tore open the envelope and took out the single sheet of paper.

'My dearest Abigail,' she read.

'Forgive me for breaking your confidence in revealing your address to Mr Minto, but please believe me when I say I have only done it after much thought and with very good reason. Mr Minto has proved to my satisfaction that he was telling the truth and could not have been the driver of the car which ran you down. More than that, he has convinced me that far from wishing you harm, he wishes to do everything in his power to undo the harm that has already been done. Please listen to him, Abigail. If nothing else I believe he can relieve you of the burden of fear you carry. Your friend who wishes only for your happiness, Serge.'

When she looked up from the letter she saw Keir had made up the fire and was washing his hands at the sink. Her heart was beating heavily, making a rhythmic rushing sound in her ears. She licked her dry lips. 'Serge said you *proved* to him you couldn't have been driving the car?'

'And I can prove it to you, if you'll let me.' He looked at her steadily as he finished drying his hands, holding her doubtful gaze, then reached again for his inside pocket, taking out what she first thought was a note book but as he opened it and handed it to her she realised it was his passport.

'As I told you last week,' he said heavily, 'when I left Mill House after breaking our engagement, I drove straight to the airport. I was—upset. I just wanted to get away as far and as fast as I could. The first available flight was via Boston, USA, and I took it.'

The page he held before her was covered in date of entry stamps, some of them blurred and undecipherable, but the one he was pointing to was clear, the name— Boston; the date—the second of September last year, the day he had told her their marriage was not now going to take place.

'There's my proof. I arrived in Boston on September

the second, the same day I called our wedding off, two days *before* you say I deliberately ran you down, and as you see there is no record of my re-entry into this country until February of this year. Do you need to check the dates?'

Abigail shook her head. That was one date she would never forget. But her mind was spinning. How *could* Keir have been on the other side of the Atlantic? It was impossible. No way could she have mistaken Keir's car lying in wait in that layby for any other, nor could she have mistaken the distinctive shape of the lumber jack's cap he wore as he'd driven it straight at her. Could this apparently incontrovertible proof of the date stamp be a forgery then? Somehow that didn't seem possible either.

She remembered her mental agony as she had lain there in hospital, how the knowledge that it was the man she loved who had done this to her was always with her, even when she was deeply sedated, remembered how close to the edge of sanity that terrible knowledge had pushed her. Perhaps her mind *had* become unhinged!

The first intimation that she had spoken her thoughts aloud came when Keir said fiercely, 'No, don't start thinking that. I'm sure everything appeared exactly the way you said—was *made* to appear that way.'

'Made to!' She stared up at him, a frown drawing her brows together as she tried to follow what he was saying.

He put the passport away in his pocket and took her hands, sliding his up her arms until he was holding her shoulders lightly. His grey eyes were very clear as he looked down into her warily upturned face. 'Abigail, I've been doing a lot of thinking and quite a bit of investigating this last week since I learned what had happened to you and what you believed was my part in it. I know *I* wasn't driving my car that day and I'm ninety-nine per cent certain who was. And I'm sure I can prove it, but I need your co-operation.'

Once again Abigail was becoming intensely aware of his closeness, of his touch stirring once-familiar longings. She shivered and drew away. 'I don't understand. What kind of co-operation?'

His hands fell to his sides and his mouth tightened at her withdrawal. 'Considering the length of time that has elapsed since it happened, I reckon nothing less than a confession will make the charge stick. Okay, so maybe I could extract that confession on my own, though I think your presence would expedite things. But I need you there so you can hear that confession with your own ears, because——' his face tightened and his eyes were suddenly bleak '—unless you do, I can't see you believing *my* word.'

He spoke as if it mattered to him, her not believing his word, but of course that was nonsense. She had meant little enough to him a year ago—his continuing affair with another woman and his impatient ending of their engagement had proved that—so what she thought of him now could matter even less to him.

But he was still maintaining his innocence, and now he claimed he knew who *had* launched that unprovoked attack on her, and Abigail found it mattered to *her*. It mattered very much. Not that it could make any difference to the fact that she and Keir no longer had any future together but she found she very much wanted to be convinced that he hadn't been guilty of that act of callous brutality.

'What do you want me to do?' she asked apprehensively.

He let out a long breath. 'I want you to come with me now. I want you to trust me.'

Alarm made her stomach feel hollow. Suppose this was just a trick to get her out of the cottage and alone with him! Her doubt and uncertainty was reflected in her eyes and as she still hesitated he said harshly,

'If you can't trust me, Abigail, then trust your friend Serge Markovitch. I discussed my suspicions with him and how I intended to get them confirmed, and he agreed to the plan. Do you really think he would have sent me here with that letter if he thought there was the slightest chance I meant to harm you?'

'Listen to him,' Serge had pleaded, and he had signed himself, 'your friend who only wishes your happiness.' She shook her head. 'No, he wouldn't. All right, I'll come.'

It was only now, as he relaxed, that she realised how tense Keir had been. 'The car's in the lane. Do you need to change?'

She shook her head again. All her clothes were shabby now, and at least the big, sloppy sweater she was wearing concealed her painful thinness and the way her slacks hung on her bony hips. 'If I can just comb my hair. . . .'

When she came downstairs again he was standing by the kitchen window, gazing out into the yard. 'I haven't seen anyone about,' he said. 'Do you have good neighbours?'

Abigail shrugged. 'They're all students from the university and very wrapped up in their own affairs so they don't bother me. They're a bit rowdy occasionally in the evenings when they throw a party, but then in the vacations they all go away and I have the place to myself.'

He frowned. 'You must get pretty lonely then.'

'Not really.' She fished her key out of her bag and opened the door. He made no move but stood there watching her with such brooding intentness that she said uneasily, 'What's the matter?'

Her question seemed to startle him out of his absorption. 'I was looking for traces of the girl I used to know, the one who lapped up adulation, who enjoyed partying. You've changed out of all recognition, Abby, if you don't find the life you're leading now lonely.'

She caught her breath at the careless callousness of his remark. 'My *life* has changed out of all recognition.' Her voice shook. 'And I shouldn't have to remind you that it was none of my choosing.'

He looked stricken. 'Hell! I didn't mean—I only wanted to know if you *were* lonely or if you were putting up a front.'

And what did he propose to do about it if she admitted it? she wondered bleakly. He couldn't put the clock back, no one could. 'I've got used to my own company and I've learned to prefer it,' she said flatly.

His mouth tightened again as he followed her out.

It was only as she walked beside him down the yard that the possibility of having to get into the black Porsche she had last seen driving straight at her occurred to her and she felt a wash of relief when the car Keir handed her into was unfamiliar, a cream Mercedes saloon, less dashing and sporty than the black car that had assumed such sinister proportions in her mind but possibly even more luxurious, so well sprung they glided over the pot holes in the unsurfaced lane. Even so, enclosed in the confined space with this man who even now had the power to disturb her, she had to make a conscious effort to preserve her habitual cloak of remoteness.

Pausing at the main road to get into the stream of traffic, Keir turned left towards the village, but when half a mile later he turned right, Abigail tensed, until she remembered this was a cut-through to the M1 avoiding the city. But to use that route they should have taken the next turning on the right, and they didn't. It wasn't until they were well past the turning that Keir began to slacken speed, and then unbelievably he was turning left between brick gateposts crowned by stone pineapples.

Marmion! The house that had always attracted her, standing well back at a slanting angle to the road in grounds made an irregular shape by the meandering stream that was its far boundary. The house which once was to have been her married home.

She whirled to face him, her cheeks ashen as the car curved round the gravel sweep to stop in front of the weathered oak front door. 'Why have we come *here*? I thought you sold the place months and months ago.'

'Or you wouldn't have stayed on in the village?' Keir's face was grim and there was a faintly bitter tone to his voice. 'I did leave instructions for it to be sold when I left for Canada—I couldn't see myself ever wanting to live in it again. But somehow when it came to it I couldn't part with it. I let it to one of my executives——' his voice hardened, '—who at this moment is out with his wife hunting for a place of their own.'

Because Keir was thinking of moving back into it himself now? She couldn't bring herself to ask, but the knowledge that he had still owned the house while she had believed he had severed his connection with the village was disturbing. And that he might be thinking of settling here again even more so.

Almost as if reading her thoughts he asked tautly, 'Does it upset you, coming here?'

He had effectively shattered her fragile self-possession and before she could even think of prevaricating a low moan of anguish escaped. 'You know it does.'

'Abigail——' The thick roughness of his voice sent a melting sensation down her spine while the warmth of his hand covering hers clasped tightly in her lap made her nerves flutter. He was so close that for a few tense moments she thought he was going to kiss her.

'Please——' She didn't wait to see if that was his intention but turned her head away sharply.

He sighed. 'You're right. This is neither the time nor the place. Come on, we have some loose ends to tie up first.'

Abigail stared at the house and knew she didn't want to go inside. He couldn't force her, could he? She'd come here voluntarily. But he was already helping her out, holding her arm as he led her towards the front door. Numbly she preceded him inside.

Whoever had been living here this last year had looked after it well, she thought. The stripped oak floor gleamed with polish, the brass bowl full of late roses on the table in the centre of the hall was burnished to a glistening shine and not a speck of dust dulled the carved staircase. The door to the left she knew led into the kitchen which overlooked the drive and the gate, and the door opposite across the hall was the dining room. Automatically she passed the bottom of the curving staircase and walked through the archway into the sitting room.

Her eyes were drawn straight away to the huge bowed window facing her where on the raised dais filling the bow stood a white grand piano—*her* piano, the Bechstein Keir had bought her as a wedding present for the marriage that never took place. Her heart lurched when she remembered Keir's pleasure in her incredulity the day it was delivered. She tore her gaze away and let it travel round the rest of the room. Incredibly nothing had changed. The same damask curtains in a rich gold colour still hung at the big bow window and at the French window. The same old-gold velvet sofas and chairs looking as if no one had sat in them since the last time she was here. Keir's cherished stereo equipment and record collection, his shelves of books. Even the tapestry fire screen covering the empty fireplace, a picture of the view from that big bow window in glowing autumn shades, stitched by Granny Lucy's skilful fingers.

That was the last piece of needlework Granny Lucy had completed before her death. Tears started in Abigail's eyes as she crossed the room to look down at it, unaware that Keir was watching every expression that flitted across her face.

Only one thing was different—the portrait hanging

over the fireplace. A portrait of herself seated at the piano. Abigail stared at it incredulously.

'It's a pity you weren't able to give Edison more sittings,' Keir said. 'He never did get you quite right.'

So this must be the portrait Keir had had commissioned soon after their engagement! Her own professional commitments had limited the number of sittings she could give the artist and she had never seen it completed.

It was like looking at someone else, someone she'd known quite well but not herself at all. Had she really once been as happy as she looked there? She supposed she must have, but it had been a false happiness, not based on reality.

'What a naive fool I was.' She turned away from the portrait and sat down.

Keir's mouth tightened as he bit back a retort and moments later the door leading off the sitting room into the study was snatched open.

'Keir! So you're back at last! It's a bit much, dragging me all the way out here then swanning off on your own.'

And here was something else that hadn't changed, Abigail thought, shrinking back into the concealing wing chair. Zena Wilde, still as beautiful as ever—her rich mahogany-coloured hair caught up in an elegant chignon, her pretty mouth petulant, her slanting green eyes gazing at Keir reproachfully—and by her proprietorial tone, still as much in possession as ever. Against Abigail's will something twisted painfully inside her.

'Where've you been anyway?' the secretary demanded, her eyes following Keir as he strolled across the carpet to the fireplace. 'I've been——' She broke off, her eyes narrowing as she caught sight of the portrait. 'Where the hell did that come from! It wasn't here when we arrived.'

'No, I brought it with me,' Keir said calmly. 'Until

now it's hung in my bedroom at my apartment in London.'

Abigail glanced at him sharply. What did he want with her portrait in his bedroom? Come to that, why had he kept it at all? And why come out with that nugget of information just now, when it was obvious Zena had never seen it before? Was he trying to say Zena hadn't been into that bedroom—hadn't slept with him?

While questions still buzzed round her head Keir suddenly leaned forward and pulled her out of the sheltering chair. 'I've brought the original along with me too.'

'You!' Zena looked thunderstruck, her voice little more than a stunned whisper, the blusher on her cheeks standing out as her face blanched.

'Why so shocked, Zena? Could it be you're afraid Abigail and I have been exchanging notes since we got together again?' Keir dropped Abigail's hand and moved towards his secretary. 'As a matter of fact we have, especially concerning your part in breaking us up.'

The tip of a pink tongue came out to circle pale lips, but Zena recovered quickly from her shock, her slanting eyes widening in bewilderment. 'Keir, I haven't the faintest idea what you're talking about. How could *I* have had anything to do with your broken engagement?'

'Perhaps we should start with the lies you fed Abigail about our supposed relationship?' he suggested softly. 'The boasts you made that you and I were lovers.'

The sideways glance Zena darted at Abigail was pure venom but her eyes when they returned to Keir's face were melting with reproach. 'But Keir, darling, we *were* lovers.' She put a pleading hand on his arm. 'Surely you're not expecting me to deny it!'

'I can't deny we slept together.'

So he was admitting it at last! Abigail closed her eyes, wondering why it could still hurt her so much.

'But it was briefly and over long before I met Abigail,' he went on, shaking off Zena's clinging hand with an expression of distaste. 'Brief because it was a relationship I regretted at once.'

'Keir!' Zena recoiled as if he'd struck her but Abigail noted the other girl didn't deny the brevity of their affair. If Zena *had* deliberately lied to her, Abigail thought, she didn't deserve any sympathy, and yet she couldn't help a sneaking pity at the wounded look on the secretary's face.

But Keir, apparently uncaring of any pain he might be inflicting, rammed his message home. 'But if I regretted it at the time, I regret it a thousand times more now. I suppose it was spite that prompted your lies, because Abigail had something that wasn't offered to you—my ring on her finger.'

'*My* lies!' Zena's voice sharpened with resentment. 'How do you know it's not Abigail who's been lying about what I'm supposed to have told her? She was always jealous of the time you and I spent together.'

'She was lying too about seeing you leaving my room that night she stayed here at Marmion?' he asked silkily, then his voice hardened. 'I think not, Zena. Abigail wasn't aware that I stayed up working in the study that night, but *you* knew. I suppose you heard her go to the bathroom and carefully arranged for her to "catch" you, knowing you were perfectly safe as I was out of the way downstairs.'

'You—you didn't go to bed at all?' Abigail broke in uncertainly. He sounded very certain and Zena wasn't trying to argue with his assertion.

His expression softened as he looked at her. 'Do you think I could have slept that night, knowing you were under my roof and not sharing my bed?' The intimacy of his voice sent a tremor down her spine.

'I still say Abigail's making it all up to cause trouble

between us,' Zena said harshly. 'Wives and girlfriends are notoriously jealous of their man's secretary.'

'All right Zena, let's forget the lies you fed Abigail and go on to the lies you told me.' He turned to his secretary again with an implacability Abigail recognised with a shiver. He had been just as inexorably unyielding when he had told her he no longer wanted to marry her, and though that remorselessness was not aimed at herself this time, she couldn't help feeling chilled.

Again Zena's tongue flicked out to moisten her lips. 'I don't know what you mean.'

'Oh I think you do. I can see the guilt in your eyes.' He towered intimidatingly over the girl. 'I'm talking about when I was in Canada and like a fool used *you* to keep me informed of how Abigail was faring. Maybe it wasn't an outright lie when you told me she'd moved in with another man. You just omitted the important fact that the man was a very old family friend and that her grandmother was also with her. And what else was it but a barefaced lie when you told me Abigail was off on tour again, her career going from strength to strength, when you knew perfectly well she was lying injured in hospital and was never going to play the piano again? You knew because you put her there!'

Abigail jumped with shock. Keir was accusing *Zena* of driving his car that day? Of deliberately running her down?

Something flickered in the other girl's eyes but she said coolly enough, 'Keir, I really don't know what you're talking about. All right, maybe I didn't inquire too deeply into Abigail's doings when you asked me to, but I couldn't see the point. You *had* broken off your engagement to her after all.'

'Exactly.' Keir pounced like a cat on that last statement. 'You knew I'd broken my engagement before I left for Canada, so why did you set up that supposed meeting for me with Abigail when she telephoned? Why did you tell her I'd meet her in that layby in Newton Lane?'

'Meeting? I don't know anything about arranging any meeting,' Zena denied.

'You lying bitch!' Keir's words were all the more menacing for being spoken quietly. 'For more than twelve months Abigail has believed *I* was driving the car that deliberately injured her that day, but it was you, wasn't it? You'd succeeded in coming between us, but when Abigail tried to see me you were afraid we still might get together again in spite of all your efforts. So you decided to get rid of her permanently.'

Abigail shuddered. Surely this dainty, beautiful girl couldn't be guilty of attempted murder!

'You set up that meeting and it was you who kept the appointment,' Keir went on remorselessly. 'And just in case you failed in your objective, you wore that lumber jack's cap of mine as a disguise. You baited your trap and then you deliberately ran Abigail down, callously driving off and leaving her bleeding at the roadside.'

'No!' Zena refuted hoarsely, but with a sick feeling in her stomach Abigail knew it was perfectly possible. That date stamp in Keir's passport couldn't lie so if he had been far away in Canada, the driver of his car that day couldn't have been anyone else but Zena. Driving Keir's car and wearing his distinctive cap she could easily have passed for Keir himself in those few terrifying moments.

'Keir, that's a dreadful accusation to make,' Zena persisted in her denial.

'Nowhere near as dreadful as what you *did*,' Keir came back grimly. 'I hope you sweated those first few days, Zena, wondering what Abigail was going to tell the police. The devil must have been looking after his own when she kept quiet.'

'Then why did she?' Zena said at once. 'If, as you claim, she recognised the car and the driver, why did

she tell the police she didn't? Why did she make out it
was an unknown hit and run?'

Keir's eyes narrowed. 'You followed the case very
closely for someone who denies any knowledge of it. And
God knows why she didn't tell the truth.' Abigail felt his
brooding gaze on her. 'I can only suppose it was out of
some misplaced desire to shield me, even though she
thought me capable of——' He bit off the words.

Abigail shook her head dumbly. Misplaced! As if it
had been a conscious decision! He couldn't know the
torment she had gone through, torment of spirit and
soul. And all so needlessly. If she *had* told the police
what she knew, the truth might have come out at the
time. If Zena really had been responsible, somehow
Abigail didn't think they were going to get a confession
out of her now.

'Keir, do we have to go on with this?' Her body
ached with tension. 'I . . . I'm prepared to believe now it
couldn't have been you driving that car. But even if
you're right and it was Zena who was responsible, well,
we don't have any proof, do we?'

His grey eyes seemed to sear through her, but then he
turned back to Zena. 'Oh but we do have proof,' he
said quietly, and Abigail's own surprise went unnoticed
as the slight smile on the other girl's face turned to
uncertainty.

'To have smashed Abigail's hand as badly as it did,
my car must have been going at a hell of a lick when it
hit the open door of hers, so it follows there must have
been some damage to the Porsche.'

'Is that your so-called proof?' Zena said quickly.
'You know very well the Porsche was sold not long
after you went off to Canada. On *your* instructions.'

But if her counter accusation shook Keir he gave no
sign of it. 'So it was,' he agreed. 'You must have
thought you were really home and dry then. And of
course it was in perfect condition when it was sold. I
checked.'

Abigail was as bewildered as Zena appeared to be as to the exact nature of the proof Keir claimed he had, but when he went on softly, 'It took me quite a time to track down the body-shop you used to do the repairs, but my persistence was rewarded,' she saw Zena's hands tighten convulsively on the back of the chair.

'Just the kind of backstreet outfit where they wouldn't ask too many questions, eh, Zena? Unfortunately for you he *does* keep records, and he allowed me to take a photocopy.' He slid his hand into his pocket and pulled out a sheet of paper, holding it out to the girl. 'A copy of his worksheet giving exact details of the damage and the repairs carried out, damage entirely consistent with the car hitting the open door of another at speed. You were careful to pay the bill in cash, I notice, but again, unfortunately for you, the garage man has an eye for a pretty face. He picked your photograph unhesitatingly out of several I showed him. A right little dolly, he called you. But in spite of fancying you he's willing to give evidence.'

Zena was visibly trembling. She made no attempt to take the incriminating document from him but made one last appeal. 'Keir, you can't do this to me. Not after we've worked together for so long. Not after what we once were to each other.'

'Can't I?' Even Abigail cringed at the savagery in his voice and when he grabbed her left hand, stripping the black glove from it, she tried to resist but was powerless against his ferocious strength.

'Look at it!' He dragged Abigail along with him as he grasped a handful of Zena's hair to prevent her backing away and forced her gaze down on to the mangled hand in front of her. 'Look at the damage you did. You could have killed her, you bitch. As it was you caused her unimaginable pain and not only wrecked her life but deprived the world of a very great artist.'

- Horror widened the almond-shaped eyes and Zena's face suddenly crumpled. 'I . . . I didn't mean—I never

intended to actually hurt her,' she whimpered. 'I only
wanted to frighten her off, make her think you were
rejecting her again so she'd leave you alone. I love you,
Keir. I couldn't bear to see——'

'Love! You don't begin to know the meaning of the
word.' He released his grip on her hair, pushing her
away from him in disgust. 'Will you call the police to
make the charge, Abigail, or shall I?'

Abigail stared at him, at first only able to take in the
one fact that meant anything to her—Keir was
innocent! He hadn't, as she had been forced to believe
for so long, been driving the car that had deliberately
run her down. It hadn't been Keir who had callously
driven away, leaving her trapped and bleeding by the
roadside. It was as if an enormous weight had been
lifted, releasing her spirit.

And then as his question got through to her, she
shuddered, drawing her arm away from his now relaxed
grip. What Zena had just admitted to had been vicious
and she deserved to be brought to justice. But Abigail
could still hear the anguish in the other girl's voice as
she'd declared her love for Keir. That was something
Abigail understood very well, the anguish of loving
Keir. Hadn't she once loved him herself beyond sense
or reason? And hadn't that love also driven her to take
wildly out-of-character action?

She glanced down at her maimed left hand. Could
she really blame Zena for this and feel justified in
exacting retribution? If it hadn't been for her own
shaming behaviour that day, desperately trying to see
Keir again, prepared to crawl to him, to debase her
pride and beg him to take her back on any terms, Zena
would have had neither reason nor opportunity to carry
out her wicked act.

Abigail had long ago learned that self-pity hurt no one
but herself, but she could find it in herself to pity Zena
whose one-sided love had driven her to such lengths.

'I won't be bringing any charges,' she said quietly.

'Abigail, for heaven's sake!' Keir exploded. 'After what she did——'

'No Keir. I've made up my mind. What's done is done. Putting Zena in prison won't give me back the use of my hand.'

'As far as I'm concerned they could lock her up and throw away the key,' he retorted angrily. 'As it is. . . .' He advanced menacingly on his secretary who fell back in alarm. 'You'd better get out of my sight before I do something I might regret.'

'Keir . . .' Zena made a last frightened protest.

'Out, Zena. Consider yourself dismissed as of now. And don't bother to ask for a reference.' He gave a humourless laugh. 'What could I say anyway, except that you're a good liar?'

Zena's hair had tumbled out of its chignon, her face was white and desperate. 'H . . . how do I get back to London?'

'I should care? Walk as far as the village. You might have a long wait but there'll be a bus along eventually that'll take you to Leicester station.' He clenched his fists and his muscles bulged beneath his jacket. 'Just get out of my sight, Zena, and stay out. If I ever find you within a mile of either me or Abigail, I promise you no man will ever want to look at your pretty, cheating face again.'

The dishevelled figure had a certain dignity as she walked out of the room and at the sound of the front door closing behind her Keir walked across to the bar, pouring himself a generous measure of scotch which he tossed off at a gulp. 'Why, Abigail? Why wouldn't you bring charges?'

Abigail moved away restlessly to stare out of the window at the trees that were just beginning to change to their autumn colours. She had been deeply disturbed by the morning's revelations, shaken out of the remoteness she had learned to assume to shelter her from any emotional involvement. Knowing Keir had

not after all been responsible for her wrecked life as she
had believed for so long had lifted a burden from her
spirit but hadn't dispelled her uneasiness in his
presence.

'I felt sorry for her,' she said at last in answer to his
question. 'You're not very kind to your discarded
lovers, are you?'

A dark red seeped under the tightened skin over his
cheekbones. 'Sleeping with her once or twice didn't
make us lovers,' he said angrily. 'And even if we had
been, you still expected me to be kind to her? My God,
I could have killed her for what she did to you—to us.'

'Take what you want—but don't balk at the price.
Isn't that what you're saying? Poor Zena took what
little you were prepared to give and now she's paying
for it. You took all the love she had——' Her voice
shook. 'When are *you* going to start paying, Keir?'

'You don't consider I've already paid?' he said in a
strangled voice. 'That I'm *still* paying, seeing you
standing there so—so bloody remote?'

She didn't hear him cross the room and jumped
suddenly when he seized her shoulders from behind,
turning her round to face him. 'Oh God, Abby!' His
hands kneaded the sharp bones through the thickness
of her sweater. 'You've got so thin I'm afraid you'll
break.'

To counteract the melting warmth his touch and the
tone of his voice was arousing she said bluntly, 'There
wasn't always money enough for food, and when there
was I suppose I didn't have much interest.'

He groaned. 'If only I'd *known* what was happening
to you! I feel so damned responsible——'

If he'd really cared about her none of it would have
happened anyway. All right, so her jealousy had turned
out to be unfounded, but she wasn't to know that at the
time, and Keir hadn't attempted to reassure her. He'd
walked away and he hadn't looked back, or if he had
looked back it had been only fleetingly, not caring

enough to find out for himself what was happening to her but delegating someone else to do it. Zena had admitted to being responsible for breaking them up but would they have survived as a couple anyway, when all the loving was on one side?

'I thought we'd established beyond any possible doubt that you were *not* driving that car, so I think you can be absolved of any responsibility.' She managed to keep her voice cool but she wished he would let her go before he demolished what little self-possession she had left.

Instead his grip tightened. 'When I think of all you've gone through—the pain, the wrecked career, the sheer privation—I can't *help* but feel responsible. If I'd acted differently. . . .' His hands slid round her back, drawing her into his arms. Her mind resisted but her body felt otherwise and relaxed quivering against him. 'But it's all over now, Abby. I'll make you forget. I'm going to take care of you from here on out.'

CHAPTER EIGHT

ABIGAIL closed her eyes against the intensity of her longing to give up her singlehanded struggle for survival, to lean on Keir's strength, to let him take over and dispel the soul deep loneliness of the last twelve months, the loneliness that only he could fill. She had been wrong about so many things. Keir *hadn't* betrayed her with Zena. He *hadn't* been driving the car that had callously run her down.

She had been wrong too in believing her feelings for him had died. They had merely been buried beneath the weight of her pain and disillusion and now that burden had been lifted by Zena's confession, she could no longer deny to herself that she loved him still. So wasn't there a chance she'd been wrong in her doubts that Keir had never felt more for her than a physical attraction?

Her eyelids fluttered up again, her dark eyes wary as she looked at him. 'Take care of me, Keir? I'm not a child.'

'And no way am I looking to be a father figure!' His arms tightened round her. 'I'm asking you to let me put my ring back on your finger, Abby,' he said huskily.

For a few intoxicating moments it was as if they were making up their quarrel of a year ago, as if the intervening events had never happened. If he wanted to resume their engagement, surely it must mean—

And then he shattered the mirage when he groaned, 'God, Abby, I feel so guilty! My blood runs cold when I think of all you've gone through, and it was all my fault. You must give me the chance to make it up to you.'

His words brought a return to sanity and she stiffened, pushing him away. 'I don't have the ring

158

any more.' Amazing her voice could sound so clear and steady when inside she was screaming with pain. She wanted his love and all he could offer her was his guilt!

Well if all he could feel was guilt, why should she spare him? 'I was still wearing it, you see,' she went on in the same unemotional voice that masked her hurt. 'By the time the surgeon had sorted out the pieces from broken bone it didn't seem worth saving, so I dropped it in the Thames from Chelsea Bridge.'

Although he was holding her only lightly now, she felt the deep shudder that ran through him. 'Don't! Please don't!' he begged hoarsely. 'I know we can't forget what happened but can't we put it behind us, make a new start? I'll buy you a new ring, Abby, a wedding ring this time. I want you to marry me now, as soon as it can be arranged. I want to have you near me, see nothing ever hurts you again.'

She had to fight the insidious pleading in his voice. Didn't he know nothing could hurt her more than being his wife and knowing she was no more to him than a guilty responsibility, loving him and knowing he didn't return her feelings? Keir had never used the word love, not when he'd been pursuing her across Canada, not even after she had agreed to marry him, and he didn't use it now. The word in his vocabulary had always been *want*.

She pushed more forcefully against his chest, breaking his light hold on her shoulders. 'Forgive me for not falling into your arms with gratitude Keir, but neither guilt nor a feeling of responsibility are good enough reasons to base a marriage on. You'd soon get tired of paying for Zena's sins.'

Frowning, he closed the gap between them. 'Abby, if I've given you the impression I want to marry you out of pity, then you're wrong!'

Abigail backed away, her chin lifting. 'Indeed? What else would you call it? Twelve months ago you walked away from me without a backward glance,' she reminded him. 'And you would have stayed away if it hadn't been for that accidental meeting at the concert.'

He stared at her, his throat working, then turned away abruptly and crossed to the drinks cabinet, pouring himself another whisky.

'That was no accident,' he said at last, as if only with the raw spirit inside him could he trust himself to speak. 'As soon as I got wind of that concert I knew I was going to force a meeting with you. The only reason I hadn't tried before was because like a fool I swallowed Zena's story that you'd found a new lover, had been living with him for months. And don't you think I bitterly regret walking out on you, even though at the time your jealousy seemed reason enough?'

It still hurt, the memory of how easily he'd been able to walk away from her. 'Because now you know that jealousy was neither unreasonable nor unfounded?' she retorted sharply.

'Wasn't it?' He looked at her over his shoulder and his dark glance held censure. 'Oh yes, I know now that Zena had been working on you, but you didn't trust me enough to tell me that, did you? Or to ask yourself if she might be lying. I've seen what such a lack of trust can do. . . .'

Before Abigail could let herself wonder if the accusation of not trusting him enough could be justified, he burst out, 'Hell, Abigail!' beginning to pace the room like a caged tiger. 'How *could* you have believed Zena's lies?'

'Is it so hard to understand when you'd never made any secret of your casual attitude to affairs with women?' She had only to remember he'd spent the first two weeks of their own acquaintance trying to get her into his bed! 'And *you* were quick enough to believe her on far less evidence when she told you I'd moved in with a lover,' she accused.

The grim tightening of his mouth told her the point had gone home. 'All right,' he conceded more quietly, 'I should have known you well enough to realise how out of character your moving in with a man would be. But was your opinion of me really so low that you could see me sleeping around even while we were planning our marriage?' His voice was suddenly ragged. 'You *knew* I was on fire for you. God, I only had to *think* about you to ache for you!'

'I knew you *wanted* me,' she flashed back bitterly. 'But wanting isn't the same as loving, is it?'

Keir stopped his pacing to stare at her, an arrested expression on his face. 'Isn't it?' His mouth twisted. 'I'd say wanting is very much a part of loving.'

It was, of course, as she knew to her cost. But a man could want a woman without her touching his emotions at all. 'You're telling me you once loved Zena, then?' she challenged.

Keir frowned, moving his broad shoulders irritably. 'No! You know I didn't.'

'You merely wanted her—as for a while you wanted me.' The sardonic note in her voice brought the grimness back to his jawline.

In a couple of strides he was standing in front of her, very close though not touching, his eyes glittering as they raked over her. 'Oh yes, I wanted you,' he ground out, ignoring her taunt. 'And I still want you, skinny and all eyes as you are. But do you think that's all it is, physical lust? Yes, I've wanted women before but I've never felt the slightest desire to tie myself to any one of them for life. Do you really think a man offers marriage so lightly, Abby?'

His nearness, her awareness of him was overwhelming. She felt if he touched her she would shatter into a million pieces, and yet she didn't dare back away in case such a move prompted him to do just that. Her arms rigid at her sides, her strained voice betraying the brittleness of her control, she said, 'Oh yes, I was naive enough at the time to imagine you must love me if you were prepared to marry me but I've grown up a bit since then. I only have to remember the manner of your proposal, Keir. You told me yourself that until that moment you'd had nothing more than an affair with me on your mind. At least you were honest then. You didn't pretend to feelings you didn't have. So be honest now and admit it wouldn't have entered your head to marry me if you could have had me any other way.'

His jaw moved as if he was grinding his teeth together and the tension between them was a palpable, physical thing, making her ache all over.

But he didn't deny it and she rushed on bitterly, 'There have been many times over these last twelve months when I've wished I *had* settled for an affair with you. At least I'd have been left with some kind of life afterwards, I'd still have had my career.' Her voice cracked. 'I might even have been over you by now.'

He let out a long breath and with it the tension that had held them in rigid confrontation drained away. Abigail found she could breathe normally again, even relax her clenched fists.

'Why are you still fighting me, Abby?' he asked softly, and she blinked up at him, realising too late she had lowered her guard prematurely. 'I know that for more than a year now you've believed me guilty of the most brutally callous act imaginable—deliberately injuring you and wrecking your life, and I know it can't be easy for you to adjust to the fact that you were wrong. But just how long are you going to go on punishing me for something I didn't do?'

'I'm not!' Abigail refuted the allegation vehemently.

'Are you sure?' His voice was still soft but very insistent. 'A few moments ago you asked me to be honest with you, so how about applying some of that honesty to yourself?'

Colour flared in her cheeks and she shifted uneasily. Could he be right? For so long now she had seen Keir as her evil genius, the author of all her wrongs, the man who had wiped her life bare of all that had made it worth living. Was she still, subconsciously, clinging to that image of him, even though she now knew he was innocent?

She shook her head, frowning. No, she was sure she wasn't still holding that against him. Hadn't she felt an overwhelming relief, a lightening of her spirit when she had finally learned the truth?

She became aware that he was watching her closely, his intent gaze trying to read the thoughts behind her troubled expression. His glittering eyes caught hers and he held her prisoner, willing her to submit to his magnetism.

'The feeling is still there, isn't it Abby?' he breathed. 'You're not as immune to me as you try to pretend. Come on, admit it honey. It was that devastating honesty of yours that was one of the things that set you apart from other women, made you special.'

His voice was a caress, tingling over her senses. His words seduced, his eyes drew her, his compelling attraction submerging her will. Her body remembered so well his touch, the delight of skin on skin, and craved it again. It remembered yielding softness against dominating strength and yearned to submit.

But you've been that way before! her mind screamed in protest, and she began to tremble. Loving Keir had almost destroyed her once, she couldn't let it happen again. There was nothing more destructively humiliating than loving a man who had no love to give in return, and she knew she had to fight the feelings he aroused in her to the utmost of her will.

She didn't *want* to feel. She was afraid of his attraction, of his power over her emotions. Afraid of her vulnerability if she let him close again, afraid of the need for him in her that had once had her crawling to him, begging for crumbs, her personality submerged, her self-esteem in shreds, her spirit crushed. She didn't dare to allow him to become so essential to her again.

Turning away from him she picked up the black

glove he had stripped off and tossed on to a chair and
began to work it back on to her scarred hand.

'I'm sure you mean well but I've no wish to become
an object of your charity, Keir.' She had been almost
afraid to try her voice in case she betrayed how close
she had come to capitulating to his persuasion, but it
came out surprisingly clear and emotionless. 'And now
if you don't mind, I'd like to go home.'

As she looked up she thought she surprised an
expression on his face that might have been despair but
it was gone so quickly behind a blank mask she knew
she must have been mistaken. 'Very well,' he nodded,
'I'll take you.'

'There's no need,' she said quickly. 'It isn't all that
far to walk.'

He didn't bother to reply but escorted her firmly out to
the car.

Neither of them broke the silence but as he drew to a
halt at the bottom of the lane Abigail felt impelled to
say, 'Keir, in his letter Serge said he thought listening to
you would lighten my burden. I want you to know it
has. I . . . it meant a lot to me to learn the truth. It *was*
an intolerable burden, having to believe——'

'—That I was some kind of sex maniac with
homicidal tendencies?' he finished for her bitterly. 'I'm
glad Zena's revelations removed *your* burden. I only
wish I could say the same about mine.'

Abigail's eyes flickered over him uneasily. 'What did
he mean? What burden could Keir be carrying? Other
than his guilt, she supposed.

And she didn't want to know about that! Abruptly
she averted her gaze and pressed the door catch.
'Goodbye, Keir,' she said with finality and slipped out
of the car, walking away from him up the yard without
looking back.

The pile of completed manuscript on the right-hand
side of the small desk salvaged from her grandmother's

home was growing satisfyingly thick but Abigail was aware of nothing but the urgency of capturing the music inside her head as her pen moved swiftly over the closely lined paper. Her head bent over her self-imposed task she was oblivious to the wisps that had escaped the piece of string with which she had impatiently tied back her tawny fair mane of hair and she was still wearing the sloppy sweater and loose-fitting slacks she had worn the day before, because she had forgotten to go to bed in between.

The glass of milk she had poured for herself on waking, stiff and surprised to find herself still at her desk with the light burning where she must have fallen asleep from sheer exhaustion, stood untouched beside her left hand. A left hand no longer concealed behind the black glove she had worn for the last year to hide her disfigurement.

When she had walked back into the cottage yesterday there had been no thought in her head of the music that had been teasing her subconscious for weeks. In fact her mind had been strangely empty, as if a giant hand had tipped her upside down and dislodged everything she had ever known—or *thought* she had known—through the top of her head, wiping her consciousness clear. She had dropped her bag on to the easy chair, not even noticing that the fire in the range needed making up, and like a sleepwalker she had gone to sit at her upright piano in the little parlour. She flexed her hands over the keys as she had so many times in the past before beginning to play, but of course her left hand refused to respond, still and useless in its thin black covering.

For more than a year her damaged hand had been an irremovable reminder of what Keir had done, and so she had hidden it away. Slowly she peeled off the black glove and found she could look at it dispassionately, almost curiously.

Only the thumb had escaped damage. The first finger was foreshortened, having lost its tip altogether, and the nails of the other three fingers had regrown slightly misshapen. The scar tissue was livid against the pallid white of the undamaged areas of skin, but if the pale gold of her wrist above where the glove had been was anything to go by, the scars would surely be less obtrusive if she had let the sun to them this summer. And she had to admit the surgeon had done a remarkable job piecing together the shattered bone, replacing it where necessary with steel pins; still a bit twisted across the knuckles, but the fingers fairly straight in spite of the immobile joints. The surgeon had even told her that physiotherapy and special exercises would restore a little movement to those joints, but because it could never restore her ability to play the piano again, she hadn't bothered. Maybe she should. . . .

She felt surprised at herself at the thought. Well maybe even if she could never play again, it might be useful for everyday things if she could get back just a little use to the hand. The black glove slid to the floor and she didn't even notice it fall.

Her right hand began to move unconsciously over the piano keys, picking out a melody, developing it into a theme, and into her oddly clear mind the music expanded and grew, no longer just tantalising snatches that floated out of her reach when she tried to grasp them but full-bodied and rounded out against her inner ear, as if some invisible bolt had been drawn back to unlock the flood.

In feverish haste she left the piano and scrabbled in the desk for the box of manuscript paper, her pen beginning to fly over the lines translating the lyric poignancy of the music in her head to notes on paper. Soft, the music was at first, and tentative, like a young girl waking to love, but slowly gathering sureness until it was soaring, rising in ecstatic cadenzas, only the occasional discord in the bass warning of disillusion and pain to come.

Unknowingly she was reliving her own emotional awakening, sublimating it through the music that swelled so insistently inside her. Her conscious mind had turned away from the things she had learned that morning, accepting with relief of spirit that Keir was *not* guilty of either unfaithfulness or of wrecking her career as she had believed for so long, but refusing to examine what this meant to her, so her subconscious had taken over. She had suppressed her warring emotions—the frightening knowledge that Keir's touch could awaken all her old feelings for him, the humiliation of his offer of marriage that had been prompted merely by pity and a sense of responsibility—and so those emotions were finding an outlet in her music.

She worked on, oblivious to everything but the urgency of writing that music down, forgetting to eat, unaware of the chill that crept into the cottage when the fire died in the range, only switching on the light when it became too dark to see. Working on unremittingly until her head drooped, the pen fell from her fingers and she slept. Waking in the morning dry-mouthed and bewildered, but with the music still beating against her inner ear, she had switched off the lamp, sluiced her face with cold water and swallowed half a glass of milk before beginning again.

So absorbed was she she didn't hear the rattle of bottles as the milkman delivered the milk or, much later in the morning, the rap at the door followed by the latch lifting. Only when a deep voice behind her said, 'Abigail?' did she lift her head to see Keir standing in the parlour doorway frowning at her. And even then, so deep was she in that other world she felt no surprise or alarm at seeing him.

'You didn't answer the door,' he said, and when she still stared at him dazedly, 'Serge phoned me. He was worried. He hadn't heard from you, and when he tried

to ring you at the prep school they said you hadn't
turned up this morning.'

The school! With an effort she dragged her mind
back to the mundane matters of daily living. She should
have been at the school to give her lessons this morning.
'Oh Lord! I forgot. . . .' She glanced back at the page in
front of her, the pen still poised above it. She couldn't
leave it now.

'What were you working on with such fierce
concentration?' Keir moved closer and looked over her
shoulder.

'I started it yesterday,' she said vaguely.

He stared at the pile of completed manuscript.
'You've done all that since yesterday? You must have
worked non-stop!'

She shrugged. 'More or less.' The pen seemed to
quiver in her hand as if impatient of this interruption.

'And you haven't eaten.' He was eyeing the half-
drunk glass of milk.

She shrugged again. 'I don't remember.'

She saw his mouth tighten but felt only relief when he
turned away. Almost at once her pen was moving over
the paper again and she was oblivious to sounds of
movement in the kitchen, the grate being raked out, the
clank of the coal bucket, Keir's muffled oaths as he
struggled to light the reluctant fire, and later the sound
of cupboard doors and the fridge being opened and
closed.

Only when he said, 'There's nothing to eat in the
house!' was she aware that he hadn't left after all.

Her head came up reluctantly. 'No. I should have
done some shopping today.'

'Nothing's reaching you, is it?' he said, and she
looked at him vaguely, unaware that he'd been
watching her utter absorption for some minutes before
he'd broken the silence. 'All right, I guess what you're
working on is very important to you. I'll call Serge and
tell him you're okay, and I'll call that school of yours

and make your excuses, tell them you won't be back for a while. And what if you give me the names and addresses of the pupils who come here to the cottage so I can put them off for a while too?'

She didn't question why he should be doing this for her as she gave him the short list from her address book, but she was grateful for his understanding. The door hadn't closed behind him before her head was lowered over her desk again.

She worked on oblivious until strong hands descended on her shoulders and almost lifted her bodily from the chair. 'Come and eat,' Keir said.

'I thought you'd gone.' She blinked up at him but allowed him to lead her into the kitchen. Two places had been set at the small formica-topped table. The fire was glowing in the range and a large box of groceries stood on top of the fridge. 'You've been shopping!'

He shook his head, smiling at her. 'Somebody had to, or were you planning on starving yourself to death?' Without waiting for an answer he pushed her towards the stairs. 'Go and wash your hands,' he ordered, and obediently she did as she was told.

When she came down again he set a fluffy omelette and fingers of buttered toast in front of her. 'You cooked this on that old range?' she said when the first forkful had melted in her mouth.

He grinned. 'I've cooked on more primitive stoves than that before now,' and her eyes opened wide in surprise. Cooking for himself didn't seem to tie in at all with what she knew of his sophisticated way of life, let alone cooking for himself under primitive conditions.

They ate in silence while she pondered this new facet of the man who faced her across the table looking utterly at home, and then he produced an apple pie that had been warming in the oven. 'One of Mrs Jameson's,' he explained.

'She's still at Marmion then?' There had been no sign

of the housekeeper when Abigail had been there yesterday.

'Of course.'

Her mind veered away because she didn't want to think about Marmion, and as if sensing it Keir changed the subject.

'I'm curious, Abigail. How can you write music at that speed when you can no longer play the piano, try it out for yourself?'

'It's all there in my head. I can *hear* it.' She spoke as if she was surprised at the question. 'After all, Beethoven was stone deaf when he wrote some of his greatest music.' She smiled deprecatingly. 'Not that I'm claiming to be another Beethoven!'

'It's in your head now? That's why you seem so far away?' His eyes caught her gaze and she nodded, a tinge of colour coming to her cheeks.

'It's with me all the time, even since I got back here yesterday.' She rose abruptly from the table, breaking contact with the grey eyes that seemed to be trying to see right inside her head. But as she turned towards the parlour he caught her wrist, holding her back.

'I notice you're not wearing your glove, Abby,' he said softly.

It was her left wrist he held and his touch seemed to burn, seemed to bring sensation back into fingers that had felt none since her hand was crushed. 'No. It didn't seem—necessary any more.'

Something flared in his eyes, something that alarmed her and she tugged her hand away and fled into the parlour to her desk. But now she was aware of his presence in the kitchen, moving about as he cleared up after their impromptu meal, and it wasn't until the back door opened and closed and silence descended that she was able to lose herself completely in her work again.

It was well into the evening when he returned and this time Abigail heard him open the door. She got stiffly to her feet and faced him defensively across the width of the kitchen. His eyes went to the box of untouched groceries.

'I didn't think you'd get around to feeding yourself,' he said dryly. He held up a covered dish. 'One of Mrs Jameson's casseroles.' His expression softened tolerantly. 'Get on with your work while I warm it up.'

She went back to her desk, a strange feeling of security warming her.

They shared the delicious chicken casserole and by the time they'd finished it, Abigail's eyelids were drooping with tiredness.

'Bed for you, my girl,' Keir said briskly, pulling her to her feet.

She shook her head, her eyes wandering to the parlour door. 'It's early yet. I'll work for a bit longer.'

'You're nearly asleep on your feet,' he derided. His hands tightened warningly on her shoulders. 'Are you going to do as you're told and put yourself to bed or do you want me to do it for you?'

The shaft of awareness, the desire to feel his hands on her skin, undressing her, was shocking in its intensity, and Keir's sharply indrawn breath, the leap of flame in his eyes told her he had read it in her face. Tearing herself out of his grasp she fled upstairs as if all the devils in hell were after her, to stand rigidly with her back against the bedroom door, listening to the sounds of him moving around the kitchen, clearing up after their dinner. Only when she heard the back door open and close and his footsteps moving away along the yard did she relax and get ready for bed.

She woke with the dawn feeling well rested after a good night's sleep and was already at her desk in the parlour when Keir walked into the kitchen just before eight o'clock. He raised his eyebrows when he saw her but when she refused his offer of breakfast he merely placed a steaming mug of coffee at her elbow, made up the range and went away.

For the next couple of days the pattern was the same.

Three times a day he came, carrying coal, keeping the fire in the range alight and feeding her. And each evening Abigail was careful to take herself off to bed without prompting straight after supper.

It was on the third night as she was about to go up that the incongruousness of the situation struck her and she hesitated at the bottom of the stairs. 'Keir, why are you doing all this?' He paused in the process of carrying plates to the sink and looked at her questioningly. 'Looking after me like a nanny, I mean.'

'Because you need a nanny.' He spoke lightly but the sharp clatter when he put the plates down betrayed his tension. He turned to face her and all attempt at lightness was gone. 'What would you say if I told you it's because I love you and can't keep away from you?'

For a moment she felt as if she'd stepped out into space and she had to fight desperately hard against the apparent sincerity in his voice to regain solid ground. He hadn't loved her twelve months ago when he had so coldly and contemptuously walked out of her life, so why was he claiming to love her now? Did his guilt bite so deep he was willing to pretend? And he wasn't actually saying it even now, was he?

'I wouldn't believe you,' she said coldly. 'Pity's easily mistaken for love.'

'You think I should pity you?' He laughed although there was no humour in it. 'You told me once you were tougher than you look, and by God you were right. Oh I regret the sheer senseless waste of what Zena did to you, the pain you've had to suffer, and I still get sleepless nights thinking of you going through all that alone. But why should I *pity* a girl with your guts and tenacity, a girl with your incredible talent?'

'Talent?' she stared at him nonplussed and he gave a slightly sheepish shrug.

'I took some of your manuscript home with me last night. I don't pretend to be an expert sight-reader but I was able to play enough to know that what you're composing now is good, far better than the piece Ling Tan played at your benefit concert.'

'You *played* it?' In spite of herself excitement stirred within her. To be able to hear it, to hear if the notes she had written really did match up to the music in her head. . . .

As if understanding her sudden longing Keir said softly, 'Would you like me to play it for you now?' Without waiting for her answer he walked into the parlour and she followed him slowly.

The old upright piano lacked the tone and resonance of a good concert grand and Keir's performance was far from professional standard—though still surprisingly good—but after the first few bars Abigail listened with rapt attention, caught up in the alchemy of hearing someone else reproducing the sounds that until that moment she had only heard inside her head.

'Thank you,' she said softly when he came to the end, but it was as if invisible bonds held her and she didn't move.

The man at the piano held his breath as he looked at her, still far too thin even though he'd been feeding her up for the last few days, shadows of fatigue making dark smudges under her eyes, the rapt look on her face as if she was still listening to music he couldn't hear, and he felt near to despair of ever breaking down the barrier the last twelve months and his own crass actions had erected between them, the barrier she seemed so determined to maintain.

He wished he could take her to Marmion where he could look after her properly, but Jack Clark and his wife still hadn't found a place of their own yet. It wasn't until he saw the leap of defensive alarm in her dark eyes that he realised he'd spoken this wish aloud.

'No. I could never go to Marmion.' His suggestion had broken the spell she was under and hastily she re-erected the defences his playing of her music had temporarily lowered. 'Thank you for playing for me,' she muttered. 'I'll say goodnight now.'

But once in bed, sleep was elusive. Things Keir had said to her kept coming into her mind and wouldn't be shifted. '... *I've wanted women before but I've never felt the slightest desire to tie myself to any one of them for life ... Do you really think a man offers marriage so lightly ... Why should I pity a girl of your guts and incredible talent ... Because I love you and I can't keep away from you. ...'* Against all reason, against all she knew of him, of his attitudes, the way he had behaved in the past, he was beginning to sound terribly convincing.

And she didn't dare to be convinced! She had already accepted his help, allowing him to do things for her, and the domestic confines of the cottage had already brought them closer in a way they had never been before even during their brief engagement. She had come to rely on him these last few days, to even, she realised now, unconsciously welcome his appearances. If she once let herself believe his renewed interest in her was prompted by genuine feelings and not pity, if she let herself be deluded that he really did care, how long could she hold out against him?

A cold perspiration broke out on her skin, because hold out against him she must. Once let him breach her defences she would be lost, a cringing, cowering supplicant at his feet again. She would lose her identity, her independence of will, her pride, her self-respect. Loving Keir had degraded her once, she couldn't let it happen again.

'Because you need a nanny,' he'd said when she'd asked why he was taking so much trouble with her, implying that she needed *him*. Well she *didn't* need him. She must show him she was well able to take care of herself, even if it meant having less time to work on her music. She couldn't let him reduce her to the poor besotted creature who had handed Zena Wilde the opportunity and motive to wreck both their lives. She *wouldn't*. . . .

The next morning she ignored the familiar pull to get to her desk to begin work. She took the trouble to wear a clean, well-pressed dress and to make sure her hair was well brushed before she tied it back, and by the time Keir arrived she had the kitchen tidy, the fire glowing in the range and the coal bucket filled and was about to put the casserole she had prepared for her midday meal into the side oven to cook slowly.

He stood very still just inside the door, his eyes flicking round the room, not missing a thing, and then narrowing as they came to rest on her face. 'You wouldn't be trying to prove something, would you, Abby?' he said softly.

She found she was trembling but managed to return his stare defiantly. 'Only that I'm perfectly capable of looking after myself without your help.' She slid the casserole in the oven. 'My dinner, you see, so you can rest assured I shan't starve. And I've set the alarm to tell me when it's ready.' She indicated the clock on the kitchen table. 'I don't need you, Keir. I don't need anyone.'

'Then you're unique on this earth, Abigail.' His voice was thick as if he was fighting a despairing anger. He took a deep breath. 'Don't I even rate a thank you for *caring* if you worked yourself to death?'

She bowed her head to avoid meeting the bleakness in his eyes that unaccountably made her feel guilty, and the trembling inside her increased. But she held tenaciously to her decision. 'Of course,' she muttered. 'Thank you for going to so much trouble on my behalf. I realise how busy you must be with your own affairs, especially as you're without a secretary, and how inconvenient it must have been coming here. I'm grateful, truly, but as you see it's no longer necessary for me to take up your time.'

'I could strangle you, Abigail!' he ground out

between clenched teeth and for a moment she really did think he meant to strike her. Then the violence drained out of him.

'All right, message received loud and clear,' he said flatly. 'I shan't trouble you again.' He turned on his heel and the door snapped shut behind him.

CHAPTER NINE

As Keir's departing footsteps faded, Abigail walked through to the parlour on shaking legs and sat down at her desk. It had been more difficult than she'd anticipated, sending him away for good, but it was what she wanted, wasn't it? To be finally free of his disturbing appearances? So she couldn't understand the heavy feeling of depression that was creeping over her, the terrible sense of isolation.

She picked up her pen but overnight the music in her head seemed to have changed. Yesterday it had been beginning to lighten again, to soar after the threatening turbulence of the middle passages, echoing the lyricism of the opening movement. But now she could only hear the dark discords again, the minatory tones.

She worked on doggedly, carefully stopping to eat when her alarm clock warned her of the time, just in case Keir should take it into his head to check up on her. He didn't, and when she returned to her desk after washing up the few dishes she knew that what little she had accomplished during the morning was entirely wrong for the completed form of the work. Screwing the pages into a ball she threw them into the wastepaper basket and began again, trying to recapture the mood of yesterday.

Sometimes she was able to grasp it, but after a few phrases it would elude her again, returning to the dark chords of despair. And as exhaustion crept over her, even the dark discords began to fade. She switched off the lamp and dragged herself to bed. In the morning, when she was fresh, everything would come right again, she promised herself.

But in the morning there was only an echoing, empty silence. The music had gone, deserted her.

She'd been overdoing things, she comforted herself. It would come back, provided she didn't try to force it. Carefully keeping her mind blank she busied herself with the chores but when, raking out the ashes in the range, she heard firm footsteps approaching up the yard, her heart leapt. Keir had come back!

She leapt to her feet, looking towards the door. But it didn't open. There was a rattle of milk bottles and the footsteps began to recede. Slowly Abigail began to sweep up the ashes she had spilt in her eagerness, admitting to a crushing disappointment. She had *wanted* it to be Keir! And admitting it, the cottage seemed to be full of him; there at the sink doing the mundane washing up, there at the range, taking Mrs Jameson's latest offering from the oven, there at the piano, playing her music. Dear heaven, was she never to be free of him?

She heard the rattle of the milkfloat she had missed on its arrival, departing up the rutted lane. She heard voices and laughter as the student occupants of the other cottages left, a group of them in an old banger one of them drove and the rest on bicycles, and then there was nothing but the uncanny silence.

Perhaps if she got right away from the cottage. . . . Determinedly she collected her shopping bag and began the lengthy walk to the village, deciding while she was there to phone Serge from the public call box.

Comforting though it was to hear his caring, attractively accented voice, she realised it was a mistake to call him almost as soon as he answered.

'Keir tells me you're working the clock round on a new composition, Abigail,' he said.

'He's been in touch with you?' Abigail was unable to hide her surprise or her unease.

'He dropped in to see me this morning to let me know how you were,' the old man replied.

So Keir had left the village and gone back to London! A great wave of desolation swept over her. But what else had she expected? That he should mope around at Marmion like a lovesick schoolboy, hoping she would relent and call him back? Even if he had loved her, he wouldn't have done that, not when she had rejected his help so pointedly. And Keir had never loved her.

Did Serge know she had told Keir not to come to her cottage again? she wondered. She couldn't ask, and neither could she tell him that since she had sent Keir away, her music had dried up. That there could be a connection there was something she refused to admit.

She found herself telling Serge her composition was almost complete and promising to let him see the score to give his opinion on it as soon as possible. It was only after she had rung off that something like panic hit her. Suppose she couldn't complete it! She shook herself angrily. That was nonsense, and as soon as she got home she would prove it.

But dismayingly only silence awaited her when she returned to the cottage. Leaving the bag of groceries on the kitchen table she moved with growing desperation to her desk. Surely there had to be some way of sparking off the flow of music again. She picked up the pages she had already completed, starting at the beginning and letting her eyes travel over the notes she had written at such white-hot speed.

At first they danced before eyes, and then miraculously as her inner ear began to translate the notes her eyes were reading, she began to *hear* the music again. Unhurriedly but with a rising excitement she turned over page after page, and all the time the music in her head swelled more confidently. Her heart was racing by the time she reached the top of the last page, certain now that by going back over what she had written she had tapped again the fountainhead of her inspiration. So certain was she that the crashing silence as she reached the last written note made her feel physically sick with disappointment.

She went back to the top of the page again and found she could once again tune in to what she had written a couple of days ago, but once again as she came to the last note the music was shut off as if a door had slammed. As if she had reached an impenetrable barrier, a barrier of glass because she *knew* what should follow, but soundproof because she could no longer *hear* it.

She sat for a long time staring at the sheet of half-filled music manuscript in front of her. There was so little left to do now to bring the work to its completion, so what was the matter with her? All right, so the creative source of her inspiration had deserted her and that was frightening, but surely she could bring the work to a conclusion using her intellect alone, putting into practice all the techniques of composition she had learned?

She picked up her pen and began to work. Slowly, painstakingly the lines began to fill. It was like juggling with mathematical formulae, a Herculean labour with none of the absorption and creative satisfaction of the earlier parts of the work. She suspected too that although the musical form was working out as it should, this last movement lacked the originality, the immediacy and impact of the earlier work she had written with such white-hot urgency.

It grew dark and she switched on the light, fighting back tiredness as she wrestled with computations of chords. She wasn't aware of falling asleep at her desk but the dream was beautiful. Strong arms held her, lifted her, carried her, and she nestled into them contentedly, all inner conflicts forgotten. She wanted this dream to last forever, to feel warm and safe at last. But then she was being lowered on to something yielding and the enfolding arms were being withdrawn. She gave a moan of protest. Her eyes flickered open to see Keir's anguished face looming over her.

'Abby, I can't let you go on like this, falling asleep at your desk, killing yourself with overwork. If I hadn't come by and seen the light burning. . . .'

She looked up at him hazily, brown eyes dazed with exhaustion. Keir was in London so of course she was still dreaming. But what a seductive dream! She gave herself up to it, her lips parting on a breathy sigh of capitulation.

'Abby?' Keir voiced her name in an incredulous whisper, and with an almost painful hesitancy he lowered his head and kissed her gently, scarcely more than brushing her mouth with his, as if doubting her invitation.

Her arms crept round his neck, her fingertips testing the texture of his skin, the crispness of his hair. He felt so *real*. She sighed again, pulling his mouth down to hers, surrendering to the warmth that licked through her as his kiss deepened, the wanton response to the weight of his body as he pressed her down.

'Oh Abby, my love, my little love. . . .' He kissed her eyes, traced a line of burning kisses across her cheek, along her throat before returning to take possession of her soft mouth again. 'Oh darling, I've dreamed of this so often,' he said thickly.

In dreams nothing was impossible, not even Keir loving her. 'And now we're both sharing the same dream and I don't ever want to wake up.' She smiled up into his eyes and felt she was drowning in their clear grey depths.

She could feel him trembling beneath her hands. 'Abby, let me love you. Please let me love you. . . .'

It was as she moved against him in mute invitation that alien sounds invaded the perfection of her dream; the heavy beat of rock music as a door opened farther along the row of cottages, raucous young voices shouting their goodnights, the starting motor of a car whining before the engine reluctantly roared into life. A moth that had found its way in at the open bedroom window plopped against the parchment shade as it was drawn to the light. But the arms holding her so tightly didn't fade with the dream. They were all too frighteningly real.

'Keir, no!' She stiffened convulsively as she gasped out her protest, pushing at him, trying to twist away.

He let her go, rolling over on to his stomach. 'Abby, what are you trying to do to me?' Even muffled by the pillow his voice sounded tortured.

She sat up, staring at him, her heat thundering against her ribs. 'I thought I was dreaming,' she whispered. 'Serge said you were in London.'

'I was,' he said raggedly. 'There didn't seem much point in staying on at Marmion when you'd shut me so firmly out of your life.'

'So why did you come back?'

He groaned. 'You tell me! I just found myself bombing back up the motorway. I'd no intention of disturbing you tonight but when I saw your light burning so late, and found you fast asleep at your desk——' He raised his head and looked at her. 'Tell me, Abby, how is it you can respond to me so satisfactorily in your dreams but freeze me off when you're awake?'

Her cheeks scorched as she remembered just how uninhibitedly she *had* responded to him. Even now her body was burning up with the emotions he had aroused in her while he—she flicked a glance at his derisively mocking face—no one would believe that only moments ago he had been begging her to let him make love to her.

'Why are you doing this?' she gasped in an agonised whisper. 'Why are you so determined to humiliate me?'

'Humiliate you? Are you crazy?' He jack-knifed into a sitting position but Abigail had her eyes squeezed tightly shut and didn't see his astonishment.

'Please ... don't do it to me,' she whispered brokenly, her head bowed in supplication. 'If you have an ounce of pity in you, don't drag me through that—that degradation again.' She opened her eyes and looked down at her scarred hand. 'Don't I already have this constant reminder of my shame?'

He drew an exasperated breath. 'You're talking in riddles, Abby. What in heaven do *you* have to be ashamed of?'

'Loving you. . . .' The agonised admission was out before she could stop it. 'Wouldn't you say it was shaming to chase after a man who couldn't care less about you? To love him so much you——' She broke off, shutting her eyes again to hold back the weak tears, but even so they escaped between her lids to spike her lashes. 'All those questions you asked, Keir, but never once did you want to know why I gave Zena the opportunity to maim me, why I tried to see you again after you'd walked out on me. I was going to plead with you. I'd lost all pride, all sense of shame, and I was going to beg you to take me back. I loved you so much, was so mindlessly besotted I was even prepared to share you with Zena or any other woman who took your fancy, in spite of realising by then that you didn't love me.'

Keir's shocked, 'Oh God!' dropped like a prayer into the silence.

'How could I have damaged you so badly and never known it?' His arms reached out for her. 'No, my love, don't flinch away. I only want to hold you while we talk. Somehow I have to convince you how wrong you are. . . .'

He piled the pillows against the head of her bed and leaned comfortably against them, drawing her against his shoulder. Numbly she acquiesced and found a strange kind of comfort in his passionless embrace.

'Abby, I *do* love you, though it took me far too long and one of the stupidest mistakes of my life to realise just how much. No, hear me out.' He pressed her head back against his shoulder as she tried to deny his claim.

'You were right about one thing,' he admitted quietly. 'I wanted you from the moment I first saw you. Wanted you so much it became an obsession. And yet even then there were other feelings mixed in with my desire for you. I wanted you and yet I wanted to protect you too, even from myself. That's why I wouldn't rush you too much when we were in Canada. I wanted you to come to me of your own free will. And there was possessiveness there too. I'd never felt that about any woman before. Even though I admired your talent, was idiotically proud of you, I resented sharing you with your audiences. I wanted you all to myself. I wanted to know *I* was the centre of your world.'

His mouth twisted in self-derision. 'You see, I thought falling in love was only for teenagers, something I'd grown out of years ago, so I didn't recognise what was happening to me. I only knew that when we were together, everything was right with the world, and when we were apart I was counting the hours till I saw you again. That three-month wait your grandmother imposed—it was well nigh unbearable for me. You see very quickly you'd become—necessary to me.'

Abigail's throat ached. His description of his growing feelings was vivid, but—— 'So necessary to you that you could break our engagement? So necessary you could walk away from me without a backward glance?'

He sighed heavily. 'That's where I was not only blind but stupid. Oh I can't blame you for doubting the strength of my feelings, darling, but I was reacting to a lifetime's conditioning. Of course I realise now that instead of blindly reacting I should have questioned *why* you were suddenly jealous of Zena and my supposed relationship with her. Unfortunately it seemed enough at the time that *I* knew your suspicions were without foundation so I didn't look beyond that.'

He paused, his hand cupping her cheek, turning her face so she had no alternative but to look at him. 'Abby, I broke our engagement, not because I didn't love you but because I couldn't face seeing that love crushed to pieces by what appeared to be your totally unfounded jealousy. You see I grew up watching what my mother's obsessive jealousy was doing to my father and believing myself to be falling into the same trap scared the hell out of me. It wasn't until I'd given myself time to think out in the Canadian backwoods that I admitted to myself I'd over-reacted.'

A shadow of remembered pain flickered across his face. 'My mother's jealousy—it's a sickness. Much more than a deep-seated insecurity making her see every woman my father as much as looks at or speaks to as a potential rival. She was jealous of *us*, her own children, because we took Dad's undivided attention away from her, and at the same time she was jealous of the friendships we made when we were kids. My brothers' wives, my sister's husband. . . . Why else do you think I ducked out of taking you home to meet her while we were still in Canada? Because I knew darned well the hostility you'd have to face, the kind of hostility she levels at everyone who takes the attention and affection of those she considers her own.'

A frown pleated Abigail's brow as she considered his words. The picture he had painted of his mother was somehow shocking. Could anyone really be so possessive? She couldn't think it something Keir would make up and it must have had a profound effect on him, growing up in such an atmosphere must have coloured his own relationships, especially with women. It could explain too his shockingly abrupt rejection of Abigail herself if he thought she was displaying similar symptoms, especially as she hadn't tried to justify her suspicions let alone trust him enough to tell him of the poison Zena was spilling.

His hand moved over her face, his thumb smoothing

away the frown between her brows. 'Abby, if you think I walked away from you easily. . . . It damn near broke my heart. But by the time I was ready to admit to myself you were nothing at all like my mother, there was the width of the Atlantic between us. I tried to call you long distance but there was never any reply either from your London apartment or Mill House. Of course now I know why.' His voice shook. 'You were lying helpless in hospital. I even wrote you several times but never posted the letters. After the way we'd parted I was afraid you'd return them unopened. There didn't seem anything else I could do but ask Zena—who was still on the spot in London—to check up on how you were and what you were doing.'

His voice had been heavy with regret, but now it took on a note of anguish. 'When the bitch told me you'd got over me very nicely thank you and had moved in with a new boyfriend, I thought I'd go off my head. My brother had to keep me drunk for days to stop me flying back to London to tear you *and* him limb from limb.'

Abigail's eyes widened at his barely leashed savagery and her voice rose to an incredulous squeak as she gasped, 'You were *jealous*?'

'Murderous!' he admitted broodingly, and it was an admission that lit a light of hope in Abigail's heart, sent a wondering, tentative joy surging through her veins.

'Ironic, isn't it?' Keir said, looking down at the small, scarred hand that had crept to touch his before engulfing it gently in his own. 'I wouldn't have believed I was capable of such feelings, but then I'd never loved anyone so utterly before. There must be more of my mother in me than I realised.' He laughed, but the mockery was aimed at himself. 'I'm even jealous of Serge, your affection for him, your trust in him.'

'Oh Keir. . . .' Abigail looked up at him with troubled eyes. 'I should have trusted you, shouldn't I? If I had it would have saved us both from untold suffering.'

His mouth swooped to silence her. 'No more looking over our shoulders, Abby. No more self-recriminations or regrets. I love you, my darling. I need you to make my life worth living again. All I ask is that you believe it.'

Her mouth trembled and her eyes shone with unshed tears, tears of such happiness her body seemed too frail to contain it. 'Yes,' she whispered. 'I believe you, Keir.'

'Thank you.' There was a deep humility in his voice and as he rested his forehead against hers she watched wonderingly as his eyes too filled with tears and one escaped to trickle down his cheek.

She kissed it away. 'I love you too, Keir, and I very much want to be your wife.' Her voice shook with emotion. 'All I ask is that you never stop loving me.'

'You still think that's possible? The healing starts here and now, my love,' he said huskily, his arms tightening round her, one hand moving possessively to her breast. 'Time enough in the morning to see about making it legal but we have a wasted year and a whole lot of terrible memories to make up. Tonight I want to show you just how much I need to have and hold you, to love and cherish you.'

And Abigail, knowing how much she needed his loving and cherishing, gave herself up to his lovemaking with a joyful eagerness that was entirely natural.

When the first fingers of sunlight stealing through the window woke her, she was still in his arms. She lay watching the pale light stealing across the room feeling a content and serenity she had never experienced before. It was the dawn after a long, dark night for both of them, a glorious dawn because in Keir's arms she had learned there was no greater glory than loving and knowing herself loved deeply in return. Tenderly she watched Keir's sleeping face, the strong lines softened to a boyish vulnerability. He had made music for her last night, a great crashing symphony of fulfilled emotion. Even now there were echoes of it ringing in her head.

She lay still as the music swelled and grew, and then smiled to herself as she slid carefully out of his sleeping embrace without disturbing him and slipped on a robe to cover her nakedness. Moments later she was at her desk in the parlour, her pen flying across the manuscript paper.

The sun was considerably higher when a sound behind her made her turn.

'Abby?' Keir was watching her uncertainly and she knew he was afraid she had slipped away from him behind her defences again.

She added the final few chords to the page then stood up, smiling at him brilliantly.

'It's finished.' She curled her arms round his neck, leaning on his strength. 'When I sent you away, you took my music with you,' she explained softly. 'But last night you brought it back again. I had to get it down before——'

'Before what?' he prompted, and she knew he still wasn't sure of her.

'Before I tell you again how much I love you. Before I let you take me back to bed to apply some more of that healing, Dr Minto,' she suggested mischievously, and his face cleared.

He swept her up in his arms and carried her upstairs, dropping her on the bed and following her down to pin her helplessly beneath his weight. 'I reckon you're going to be writing an awful lot of music if that's the effect my loving has on you,' he threatened.

'Mmmm. Remind me to get in a good supply of manuscript paper, darling,' she murmured, brushing her mouth over his bare shoulder.

And then there was no thought in her head for anything but the very different kind of music they were making together.

THE END

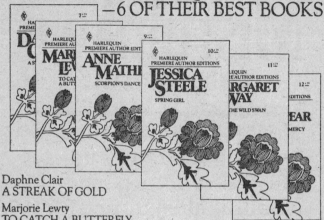

Share the joys and sorrows
of real-life love with
Harlequin American Romance!™

GET THIS BOOK
FREE as your introduction to
Harlequin American Romance —
an exciting series of romance
novels written especially for
the American woman of today.

Mail to:
Harlequin Reader Service

In the U.S.
2504 West Southern Ave.
Tempe, AZ 85282

In Canada
P.O. Box 2800, Postal Station A
5170 Yonge St., Willowdale, Ont. M2N 6J3

YES! I want to be one of the first to discover
Harlequin American Romance. Send me FREE and without
obligation *Twice in a Lifetime*. If you do not hear from me after I
have examined my FREE book, please send me the 4 new
Harlequin American Romances each month as soon as they
come off the presses. I understand that I will be billed only $2.25
for each book (total $9.00). There are no shipping or handling
charges. There is no minimum number of books that I have to
purchase. In fact, I may cancel this arrangement at any time.
Twice in a Lifetime is mine to keep as a FREE gift, even if I do not
buy any additional books.   154 BPA NAZJ

Name   (please print)

Address   Apt. no.

City   State/Prov.   Zip/Postal Code

Signature (If under 18, parent or guardian must sign.)

This offer is limited to one order per household and not valid to current Harlequin
American Romance subscribers. We reserve the right to exercise discretion in
granting membership. If price changes are necessary, you will be notified.

AMR-SUB-1